Our Father

Our Father

by

Clifford Pond

Foreword by Peter Lewis

Grace Publications

GRACE PUBLICATIONS TRUST
139 Grosvenor Avenue
London N5 2NH
England

Managing Editors
J. P. Arthur, M. A.
H. J. Appleby

ISBN 0 94646 243 7
© Clifford Pond 1996

Distributed by
EVANGELICAL PRESS
12 Wooler Street
Darlington
Co. Durham DL1 1RQ
England

Cover design by H. J. A.

Printed in Great Britain by The Bath Press, Avon.

To John and Andrew, two most excellent fathers

Contents

Foreword

'You are what you eat' has become a popular catch-phrase in recent years. I imagine no-one takes it too seriously while getting the message nonetheless. Nearer the mark might be 'You are what you read'. In the world at large, corrupt literature is likely to breed corruption in the lives of those who read it; a constant diet of shallow, superficial literature is likely to reinforce shallow, superficial attitudes and even prejudices and there is a great need of more serious thoughtful writing and more serious thoughtful reading to go with it!

In the Christian church too, there is a need for good, wholesome, thoughtful literature. We have too much that is sensational, doubtful and downright harmful. *We need more books like this one which is thoroughly biblical, constantly pastoral and always devotional. In it Clifford Pond unites a pastor's care, a Bible teacher's knowledge, and a fine Christian leader's real devotion.*

I am happy to commend this book, written in retirement by Clifford.

Peter Lewis
Nottingham

Introduction

This book has been brewing since 1951! Three years into pastoral ministry and I was breaking down fast. A friend took me to a convention where a preacher's subject was 'The forgotten doctrine of evangelicals' which he said was the Fatherhood of God. As I learned to apply that message to myself the effect was spiritual restoration, and this was gradually reflected in physical and mental relaxation and liberty. The breakdown was far from pleasant, but as with so many experiences in life, the Lord was teaching me a lesson I have been able to use to help others. Pastoral ministry has convinced me that the Fatherhood of God is still a forgotten doctrine. Even where it is remembered it is seldom applied effectively to daily thought and action. This neglect results in a lamentable loss of peace and joy.

Perhaps one reason for this failure is over re-action to the notion of a universal fatherhood taught with depressing regularity by popular religious leaders. This is the idea that we are all naturally children of God because he created us, and that consequently we have no need of a special experience to have a close relationship with God as our Father. The result, according to this teaching is that everyone without exception will eventually go to heaven and none will suffer eternally for their sin. We must not allow ourselves to be robbed of the true evangelical experience of God as our heavenly Father for fear of being tainted with such false teaching. If this book helps to rescue the Fatherhood of God from the hands of those who abuse it or neglect it, I will be grateful.

I would not want to say a word to undermine anyone's delight in the great fact of God's awesome holiness and his sovereignty in creation, providence and redemption. There is nothing in the world more liberating than taking such teaching seriously; but in honesty I have to admit that it is possible so to emphasise the transcendence of God that he becomes out of the reach of an intimate personal relationship.

A hymn writer reminds us:

> Yet I may love thee, too, O Lord, Almighty as thou art,
> For thou hast stooped to ask of me the love of my poor heart.
> (Frederick W. Faber).

God makes it possible for us to know him as our heavenly Father who otherwise would be unknowable. Praise him that he is not 'an unknown God' (Acts 17:23).

Fashions in Christian thought change about as rapidly as teenage clothes. Within a generation we have seen 'Jesus People' with their emphasis on love and liberty, and a 'charismatic' movement with its emphasis on the Holy Spirit, spiritual gifts and joy in the Lord. This tendency to fragment the Trinity is far from helpful and is one of the reasons for the present confusion in the evangelical scene. Undue emphasis on one of the three persons of the Trinity always leads to distortion of the truth and the neglect of the other two. The result is a serious lack in our personal spiritual experience and in the life of the churches. We need to be Trinitarian believers giving equal honour to the Father, the Son and the Holy Spirit. Such a balanced approach will have a beneficial effect on our evangelism, our worship and our personal spiritual stability.

So am I violating this principle of equal honour to the three persons of the Trinity in a book that singles out our relationship to the first person — the Father? You must judge! Any doctrine taken in isolation or to extreme becomes a heresy. My defence is that I am doing what I can to redress the balance.

There are five senses in which God is spoken of as Father:

1) the first person of the Trinity — Matthew 28:19

2) the God and Father of our Lord Jesus Christ — Ephesians 1:3

3) the creator of the world — 1 Corinthians 8:6

4) the founder of the nation of Israel — Deuteronomy 32:6

5) the one who gives spiritual life to all believers and adopts them into his family — Romans 8:15-16.

This gives us some idea of the scope and richness of our theme. So broad is the scope that I have limited myself in this book almost entirely to direct biblical references to the Fatherhood of God.

It is a sad commentary on modern life that there are hazards in speaking of God as our Father to people of our generation. Many children's concept of fatherhood is warped by bitter experience of neglect, abuse or brutality. Some children are subjected to such harsh, unjust treatment that they are in constant craven fear. Others have absentee fathers, either because they are never at home, or if they are, exercise no responsibility for their children's development, leaving it all to mothers. There are other fathers who would never dream of abusing their children whom they love intensely, but that love is shown in easy tolerance without effective guidance or correction. I pray that my heavenly Father will be pleased to make himself a true father to many who have suffered.

Sensing the dangers of changing fashion, Tom Smail has written 'The Forgotten Father' in which he works out the necessity to discern the Father's place in the Scriptures and in a believer's experience. I hope it is not presumptuous of me to say that here I am trying to build on Tom Smail's foundation and to take the practical outworking a little further. More recently Sinclair Ferguson has also written a heart warming 'Children of the living God' which is a practical help to the ongoing experience of the amazing privilege of an intimate relationship with God.

The Fatherhood of God is not only a doctrine to be believed and defended, it is a relationship into which every believer enters and which every believer is intended to enjoy. If some struggling child of God is helped to share that enjoyment with me through the reading of this book I will be amply rewarded.

First let us be sure we are God's children and then we will explore together what it means to have the eternal God as our heavenly Father.

1.
Our Father's children by Spiritual birth

How then do we become children of God? To many people such a question is nonsense; they would ask, how can we 'become' what we are? In their view the moment we become human beings we are children of God and continue to be so until we die. We should not dismiss this notion out of hand; there is a sense in which we are God's children because he made us and gave us life. Paul accepted this idea as the basis of his argument that God is a person and not a thing. He quoted a secular poet of his day who said that 'we are his (God's) offspring'. If that is so, Paul reasoned, then God himself must be a person like his offspring (Acts 17:28-29). So there is a sense in which simply by creation we are God's children. This is the only basis, apart from the gospel, upon which those who strive for peace in the world can make their appeal.

Natural birth

Since God made us all we belong together and ought to find ways of living together in harmony. This is a natural argument and is valid so far as it goes, but it suffers from a fatal weakness. It is doomed to failure because it is addressed to people who are powerless to respond to it with any substantial degree of success. The reason for this is that we are all born as 'fallen' people into a world of 'fallen' people. Human nature is flawed as David the psalmist wrote:

> 'Surely I was sinful at birth, sinful from the time my mother conceived me' (Psalm 51:5).

This has no reference to sexual intercourse, which is God's gift within a marriage relationship. It refers to the sinful nature which we all inherit, and because of this any appeal to human brotherhood to improve human conduct must fail.

The claim of New Age thinkers goes further than our being children of God by natural birth. To them we are not merely God's children — we are gods! Some gods! This teaching does not elevate human beings, but, since God is said to be literally everything, we are no more and no less divine than earthworms or snakes! In practice these so-called gods are not to be envied, for they are occupied in a constant search for fulfilment and perfect bliss. Not only so, their whole notion of reincarnation carries with it the same admission that we are as yet by no means perfect. According to this idea, after death we return to this life in a higher or lower form than we were before. We must reject that teaching in the light of Scripture, for example:

'... man is destined to die once, and after that to face judgement' (Hebrews 9:27).

It is obvious we are imperfect people and the Bible makes it clear this is because we have a sinful nature. We have to say with Paul the apostle:

'I know that nothing good lives in me, that is, in my sinful nature...' (Romans 7:18).

We are beginning to see why it is so important for us to be 'born again' (John 3: 3,7), which is nothing less then the implanting within us of an altogether new kind of life — a new nature. This is important for the state of society because there is no hope of improvement in human relationships without it. A society of people living by the old nature alone cannot produce morality, respect for people, property or justice. But more than this the 'new birth' is the only means by which we can enter into a love relationship with God and be made fit for an eternity of enjoyment of fellowship with him. Through the new birth we enter the family of God now, and that is the family which will populate the new heaven and new earth (2 Peter 3:13).

Spiritual birth

So how does this new birth come about? In spiritual experience everything can happen in a moment of time — the Philippian jailer may be such a case (Acts 16:16-34). We have no evidence of the Holy Spirit at work in his life before the earthquake burst open the prison. The jailer's treatment of the apostles suggests a hard-bitten, godless mind and heart, but before the night was over he was a humble, gentle child of God. The details are infinite in variety but a host of people since then have been blessed by the instant work of the Spirit. For them the whole process has been contracted to a sudden transformation, while for others the time involved may be many weeks, months, or even years.

We can understand this by likening it to the time span between conception and when the baby is born in the natural process. There is often a similar time lapse between the moment the Holy Spirit begins his work in us, giving us new life, and the time later when we become conscious that we are God's children — our spiritual birth. We call the beginning of the Spirit's work regeneration which sooner or later will result in spiritual birth.

We do not know when the Spirit's work begins:

> 'The wind blows wherever it pleases. You hear its sound but
> you cannot tell where it comes from or where it is going. So
> it is with everyone born of the Spirit' (John 3:8).

But there comes a time when we turn to God away from our godless life, and trust completely in Jesus Christ for pardon and every other spiritual blessing. We must not press this comparison with the process of natural birth too far, but it can be helpful in trying to understand how we become children of God.

How it happens

The Spirit has an endless variety of ways in which he begins his work. If we have been familiar with the Bible and surrounded by Christian influences there comes a time when we know God is speaking to us; it may be through our regular bible reading, or through sermons at church or the informal conversation of a Christian friend. In this case we will readily understand the feelings of spiritual need that accompany the new birth and we will know that we must turn to Jesus Christ as the only answer to our need.

If we are unfamiliar with Bible teaching the Spirit's work may begin with a feeling of dissatisfaction. Perhaps we question life itself and its meaning; or our conscience gives us a sense of guilt which we cannot erase from our minds; perhaps some event in life makes us feel totally inadequate and we realise a need of strength beyond our own. For example, a woman's husband suddenly leaves her without warning, a wife leaves her husband to go off with another man, a man is made redundant or a mother hears that her soldier son has been wounded in battle. Such traumatic experiences have often led to a deep spiritual experience. Whatever the cause we become sensitive to spiritual things. The first effect may be resistance to any suggestion we are becoming 'religious' and often a first sign of the work beginning is irritation, and even anger. We may be a puzzle to ourselves and to our friends; neither we nor they can explain what is happening to us.

By strange coincidences we are brought in touch with the Christian faith; we discover a neighbour or friend at work is a Christian; some Christian literature comes our way; or we have an urge to go to church. One way or another, though we may not realise it, the Holy Spirit is leading us gently but firmly to the point where we see Jesus Christ as the answer to our need, and we are enabled to trust him as our Lord and Saviour. This is how we become children of God, we are 'born again.' The soil of our hearts was prepared by the Holy Spirit to receive the word of God:

> 'For you have been born again, not of perishable seed, but of imperishable, through the living and enduring word of God' (1 Peter 1:23).

> 'Every good and perfect gift is from above, coming down from the Father... he chose to give us birth through the word of truth...' (James 1:16-17).

This is life from the dead —

> '... you were dead in your transgressions and sins, in which you used to live... But because of his great love for us, God, who is rich in mercy, made us alive with Christ...' (Ephesians 2:1-5).

Becoming children of God is clearly distinguished from natural birth in the Scriptures:

> '... children born not of natural descent, nor of human decision, or a husband's will, but born of God' (John 1:13).

This shows us once for all that no one becomes a child of God because of natural birth, belonging to Christian parents or living in a certain nation or 'Christian' area or group. The only possible way is spiritual birth and this is the work of God's Holy Spirit. The words of Jesus cannot be reasonably misunderstood —

> 'Flesh gives birth to flesh, but the Spirit gives birth to spirit' (John 3:6).

It is when we are led by the Spirit to trust in Jesus Christ alone that we become children of God. The apostle Paul wrote:

> '... those who are led by the Spirit of God are sons of God' (Romans 8:14).

> and, 'You are all sons of God through faith in Jesus Christ' (Galatians 3:26).

This faith is our conscious, positive response to the gospel. We are called upon to turn from our sinful condition and to trust in Christ alone for forgiveness, acceptance with God and power to overcome sin in our lives. Nevertheless, we would never have been awakened to our need but for the prompting of the Holy Spirit, nor could we repent and believe except by his enabling. Repentance and faith (Acts 20:21) are not the means of life, but the evidence that we have spiritual life, that we are children of God.

2.
Our Father's children by Spiritual adoption

We become children in a family either by natural birth or by a process of adoption; in each case there is the wonderful potential of a growing love relationship between parents and children. The remarkable thing is that we become children of God both by birth and by adoption!

You may wonder why we need to be adopted into God's family if we have already been born into it. The answer is that this broadens still further our understanding and experience of what it means to be a child of God; it gives us further grounds for assurance that this privilege is indeed ours; and, above all, it displays the amazing mercy and generosity of God in making us his children.

Before we think about spiritual adoption more closely let us compare it with spiritual birth:

Spiritual birth	Spiritual adoption
a new nature	a new position
a new life	a new set of privileges
inward experience	legal standing
leading outward	leading inward

These two things are clearly distinguished by the apostle John:

'... to all who received him (Jesus Christ), he gave the right to become children of God — children born not of natural descent, nor of human decision or a husband's will, but born of God' (John 1:12-13).

John speaks first of 'the right to become children of God'. We do not
speak of a child born into a family as having the right to become a
child of that family, but when all legal procedures for adoption have
been followed then a child has the right to belong to his or her new
family. Then the text goes on to say that the same people who have
the 'right' are also born of God. In his first letter John exclaims:
'How great is the love the Father has lavished on us, that we should
be called children of God!' (1 John 3:1).

What we were

Adoption is best understood in the light of our situation before we
were taken into God's family. There is a clear illustration of this
from the people of God in Old Testament days. He founded Israel
as a nation and the apostle Paul tells us that this amounted to a kind
of adoption '...the people of Israel. Theirs is the adoption as sons...'
(Romans 9:4). We can get an idea of what Paul meant from the
prophet Ezekiel:

> '... This is what the Sovereign LORD says to Jerusalem: Your
> ancestry and birth were in the land of the Canaanites; your
> father was an Amorite and your mother a Hittite. On the day
> you were born your cord was not cut nor were you washed
> with water to make you clean, nor were you rubbed with salt
> or wrapped in cloths. No one looked on you with pity or had
> compassion enough to do any of these things for you.
> Rather, you were thrown out into the open field, for on the
> day you were born you were despised. Then I passed by and
> saw you kicking about in your blood, and as you lay there in
> your blood I said to you, 'Live !' (Ezekiel 16:2-6; see also
> Deuteronomy 7:7-8; 32:9-10).

Those people were originally pagan and corrupt. There was nothing
attractive in them to make God love them or even look twice at them
— but he did.

When we come to the New Testament we find our original state
described in equally unflattering language:

'You belong to your father, the devil, and you want to carry out your father's desire. He was a murderer from the beginning, not holding to the truth for there is no truth in him...' (John 8:44).

'As for you, you were dead in your transgressions and sins, in which you used to live when you followed the ways of this world and of the ruler of the kingdom of the air, the spirit who is now at work in those who are disobedient. All of us also lived among them at one time, gratifying the cravings of our sinful nature and following its desires and thoughts. Like the rest. we were by nature objects of wrath' (Ephesians 2:1-3).

We were under the wrath of God because we were children of Adam who first sinned against God and was driven from his presence (Genesis 3). By natural birth, so far from being children of God, we share the characteristics of the evil one, and the same condemnation that falls on all of Adam's descendants; 'Sin entered the world through one man and death through sin, and in this way death came to all men' (Romans 5:12). Our natural state and condition is one of spiritual poverty because we are separated from God; of condemnation because we are under the wrath of God; and of helplessness and hopelessness because we are totally unable to help ourselves and no one in the whole universe can help us — our only hope is in the mercy of God.

Great mercy

Adoption arises entirely and only from the love and mercy of God:

'Praise be to the God and Father of our Lord Jesus Christ...
For he chose us in him before the creation of the world to be
holy and blameless in his sight. In love he predestined us to
be adopted as his sons through Jesus Christ in accordance
with his pleasure and will' (Ephesians 1:3-5).

It is as though the 'legal documents' were drawn up in eternity, before creation, before the fall, before we sinned and certainly before we believed. The love that motivated the choice has not wavered despite every provocation from us to do so. But what were the terms of adoption?

Let us trace the process in five stages.

First,   God declared that those to be adopted were transferred from union with Adam to union with Jesus Christ. Their adoption is 'in Christ' — 'in the One he loves' (Ephesians 1:3,6).

Second,   Their sin and all its consequences would be blotted out by the death and resurrection of Jesus Christ '... just as through the disobedience of the one man the many were made sinners, so also through the obedience of the one man the many will be made righteous' (Romans 5:19).

Third,   They will be given a new nature by the Holy Spirit enabling them to desire and to receive the benefits of adoption (John 1:12-13).

Fourth,   The moment they trust in Christ they begin to enjoy the privileges of adoption, 'Because you are sons, God sent the Spirit of his Son into our hearts, the Spirit who calls out, "Abba, Father" (Galatians 4:6).

Fifth,   The Holy Spirit goes on giving them assurance that they are the children of God, 'The Spirit himself testifies with our spirit that we are God's children' (Romans 8:16).

Division

The only fly in the ointment is the fact that our adoption into God's family creates a division between us and those who are outside that family:

'How great is the love the Father has lavished on us, that we should be called children of God! And that is what we are!

The reason the world does not know us is that it did not know him' (1 John 3:1).

This is always painful, especially when it involves close friends of long standing or members of our natural family. But Jesus Christ warned us it would happen:

'Do not suppose that I have come to bring peace to the earth. I did not come to bring peace, but a sword. For I have come to turn a man against his father, a daughter against her mother, a daughter-in-law against her mother-in-law — a man's enemies will be the members of his own household. Anyone who loves his father or mother more than me is not worthy of me; anyone who loves his son or daughter more than me is not worthy of me' (Matthew 10: 34-37).

Becoming a Christian does not destroy our natural affection, and our new situation needs to be handled with sensitivity. One thing is certain, it is quite wrong for Christians to cut off all former friends and relations; how then could we witness to them? Let us also remember that our Lord promised that:

'... no one who has left home or brothers or sisters or mother or father or children or fields for me and the gospel will fail to receive a hundred times as much in this present age (homes, brothers, sisters, mothers, children and fields — and with them, persecutions) and in the age to come, eternal life' (Mark 10:29-30).

No Christian should lack the blessings and benefits of a spiritual family in the life of a church.

Nothing should be allowed to affect our sense of wonder and amazement at the love our God and Father has lavished on us. When Adam was first created, he was 'the son of God' (Luke 3:38), he was in the unblemished image of God and enjoyed constant fellowship with him. He lost all this through sin, and we likewise, but in Jesus Christ we have that image restored and that fellowship re-established. The Son of God, Jesus Christ, came to make us sons of God, and when he returned to heaven he asked the Father to send his Spirit to us. He said, 'I will not leave you as orphans' (John 14:18). The Holy Spirit would make possible a continuing experience of the Father's love.

Paul could scarcely contain his joy and thanksgiving when he wrote about our adoption into God's family; 'to the praise of his glorious grace which he has freely given us in the One he loves' (Ephesians 1:6). And we have already seen that the apostle John was of the same mind (1 John 3:1).

Then follow all the benefits and privileges of belonging to God's family: his provision for our needs, access into his presence, his protection, the inheritance and so much more. Be sure you are born again, adopted into this world-wide family; if you are, then come along with me to enjoy some of these heavenly blessings.

3.
Our Father's children know they are his

Before we explore our wonderful relationship with God as children to a Father, we need to be *sure* that we are his children. Many people lack this assurance; they seek it, but for various reasons it eludes them. If we rightly understand what it means to be born again and to be adopted into God's family, we will be well on the road to 'full assurance of faith' (Hebrews 10:22).

The new birth and assurance

Our assurance that we are true Christians should be based primarily on the promises of God contained in his word such as:

> 'I tell you the truth, whoever hears my Word and believes him who sent me has eternal life and will not be condemned; he has crossed over from death to life' (John 5:24).

> 'You are all sons of God through faith in Jesus Christ' (Galatians 3:26).

The question is, how does it come about that we are now trusting in Jesus Christ when the majority of people around us reject him completely? If they think about these things at all they rely on themselves to escape from the wrath of God. Is it because we are more intelligent than others or because we are morally better than others? Of course not! There is only one explanation of our faith in Jesus Christ, the Holy Spirit has begun his work in us (Philippians 1:6). When we understand this, we can rest on all the assurances God gives us in the Scriptures about those who trust in Christ:

> '...whoever believes in him shall not perish but have eternal life' (John 3:16)

'Everyone who believes that Jesus is the Christ is born of God...' (1 John 5:1).

Another way to obtain assurance is to draw a parallel between the signs of natural life and spiritual life, like this:

Signs of natural life	Signs of spiritual life
breathing	prayer (Acts 9:11)
hunger	appetite for the Bible (Psalm119:97)
feelings	sense of sin (John 16:8)
desire for comfort	sense of God's love (Romans 5:5)
thinking naturally	thinking spiritually (Romans 8:5-6)

The apostle John adds to this evidence in his first letter. He tells us toward the end that the very reason why he has written the letter is that his readers might know they have eternal life (1 John 5:13).

He shows how they can see in themselves the evidence of this new life:

'This is how we know who the children of God are, and who the children of the devil are: Anyone who does not do what is right is not a child of God; nor is anyone who does not love his brother' (1 John 3:10).

'We know that we have passed from death to life, because we love our brother. Anyone who does not love remains in death' (1 John 3:14).

'Anyone who believes in the Son of God has this testimony in his heart' (1 John 5:10).

'We know that anyone born of God does not continue in sin...' (1 John 5:18).

If we love the Lord and his people and if our great desire is to be rid of sin and live a holy life pleasing to our Father, then we are children of God.

This evidence is confirmed by the Holy Spirit as Paul says: 'The Spirit himself testifies with our spirits that we are God's children' (Romans 8:16). When a child works out a problem in maths and writes down the answer he or she may be reasonably certain the answer is correct. But then the teacher examines the work and puts a tick under it meaning 'your conclusions are right'. Similarly, the Holy Spirit gives us a deep inward conviction that what we hope and believe about ourselves is indeed the truth and our minds and hearts are at rest.

Any father knows the thrill when a little son or daughter comes to the momentous realisation 'You're my Daddy, aren't you?' So it is that the Holy Spirit gently leads us on until we can say to God, 'You're my Father, aren't you?' — that is heaven on earth!

Nothing in the whole world can ever change the identity of our natural father. That relationship is totally incapable of being erased however much anyone may try to do so or for whatever reason. In the same way nothing can alter our relationship with God as our Father. The people of Israel in Old Testament days grieved God, were unfaithful to him and sinned against him constantly, but nothing could change the fact that they were his children. God's love for them is expressed in extraordinary language:

'When Israel was a child, I loved him, and out of Egypt I called my son. But the more I called Israel, the further they went from me. They sacrificed to the Baals and they burned incense to images. It was I who taught Ephraim to walk, taking them by the arms; but they did not realise it was I who healed them. I led them with cords of human kindness, with ties of love; I lifted the yoke from their neck and bent down to feed them. Will they not return to Egypt and will not Assyria rule over them because they refuse to repent? Swords will flash in their cities, will destroy the bars of their gates and put an end to their plans. My people are determined to turn from me. Even if they call to the Most High, he will by no means exalt them. How can I give you up, Ephraim? How can I hand you over, Israel? How can I treat you like Admah? How can I make you like Zeboiim? My heart is changed within me; all my compassion is aroused. I will not carry out my fierce anger, nor will I turn and devastate Ephraim. For I am God, and not man — the Holy One among you. I will not come in wrath' (Hosea 11:1-9).

We may at times begin to wonder if God will renounce us because of our failures and shortcomings — but we must learn to rest in the reality of this relationship with God as our Father, which is eternal because God is eternal.

If anyone abuses this teaching and goes on loving sin without regret, presuming on God's mercy, that person is proving that he or she was most probably not born again because the very nature of our spiritual life is love of holiness. As Peter said we 'participate in the divine nature' (2 Peter 1:4). This is why the apostle John can write 'No one who is born of God will continue to sin, because God's seed remains in him; he cannot go on sinning because he has been born of God'(1 John 3:9).

Adoption and assurance

Assurance is also one of the great blessings of adoption. We can draw this confidence from what the Bible says about those who trust in Jesus Christ, for example:

> '... giving thanks to the Father, who has qualified you to share in the inheritance of the saints in the kingdom of light. For he has rescued us from the dominion of darkness and brought us into the kingdom of the Son he loves' (Colossians 1:12-13).

The words of God in Scripture are our qualification and they give us a right to the privileges of God's children. We do not have to try to be children but we do need to try to be good ones!

An adopted child might gain re-assurance from a sight of the legal document of his or her adoption. In the same way we can be assured by trusting the word of God that nothing can nullify. But there is no substitute for the day to day experience of the love and care of our Father and of a developing relationship with him on the basis of trust resulting in peace and joy.

It is gloriously possible not only to be a child of God, but also **to know** that the eternal God is indeed our Father in heaven.

4.
Our Father is first

We must begin by considering the Father as the first person of the Trinity — Father, Son and Holy Spirit. You may ask why it should be necessary to do such a thing in a book that promises to deal with practical matters. The answer is that this is a very practical matter indeed! Every part of our spiritual experience is affected by our attitude to the three persons of the Trinity, and the place each of them occupies in our thinking and praying.

We can easily prove this by a visit to each of three kinds of churches where either Jesus Christ, the Holy Spirit or the Father are the most prominent in the ministry and worship. Where the emphasis is on Jesus Christ the result tends to be warm gospel preaching; where the Holy Spirit is most prominent the effect tends to physical expression and excitement; where the Father is most in mind there tends to be a greater atmosphere of reverence and solemnity. These are general tendencies and trends rather than fixed characteristics. There will be gospel preaching in a church emphasising the Fatherhood of God and there will be times of solemnity where the Holy Spirit is predominant. This is not of necessity to criticise one or other of these churches but simply to demonstrate that such matters do have a profound practical effect.

What do we mean when we say that the Father is the first person in the Trinity? We certainly do not mean that the Son and the Holy Spirit are in some way inferior to the Father. All three persons of the Trinity are God and are therefore to be worshipped with trust, love, praise and obedience. Nevertheless the Bible gives us the order of Father, Son and Holy Spirit, and if we are true to Scripture we will honour that order.

The Son — second person

So far as Jesus Christ is concerned two facts emerge. First, he is eternal as the Father is eternal. But second, he is called the Son of the Father which suggests that in some way he was derived from the Father. This is confirmed by Jesus' own statement, 'I came forth from the Father' (John 16:28 NASV). The meaning here is much more profound than simply: — **I came** from the Father; Jesus is stating that he **came out** of the Father. Our forefathers have put these facts together by speaking of our Lord's eternal Sonship. So there is order within the mystery of the Godhead — the Father is first.

The Holy Spirit — third person

Similarly the Holy Spirit is eternal, and yet at the same time an order is indicated. He is said to 'go out from' the Father (John 15:26) and he is also the 'Spirit of Christ' (Romans 8:9). Again, our forefathers put all the evidence together and said that the Holy Spirit eternally proceeded from the Father and the Son. This is a mystery we cannot understand, but clearly we are meant to speak of the three persons in the order of the Father first, and then the Son and the Holy Spirit. This is entirely in line with the baptismal declaration, 'In the name of the Father, and of the Son and of the Holy Spirit' (Matthew 28:19).

One God yet three persons

We reach the same conclusion by other routes. For instance, from the time of Abraham until Jesus Christ came, God made himself known to the people of Israel as One God:

'Hear, O Israel; the LORD our God, the LORD is One'
(Deuteronomy 6:4).

There were hints and foreshadowings of the existence of the Son and the Holy Spirit, and occasionally the Son himself appeared in what we call Christophanies (e.g. Genesis 18:1-3; Daniel 3:25), but apart from this the great emphasis was that God is One. The Israelites persistently copied other nations by falling into the worship of many gods, but they emerged from the bitter experience of captivity in Babylon as worshippers of the one and only true God. Only after that did the Son appear clearly to view when Jesus Christ was born, and then later at Pentecost the Holy Spirit was given. The order we are meant to understand could scarcely be more clearly revealed. The Father is the first person.

The Teaching of Jesus and the apostles.

The teaching of Jesus will bring us to the same conclusion. He, the Son, was sent by the Father (John 20:21) and at all times he gave honour to the Father (John 8:49; 12:28). His words, works and commission were from the Father:

> '... the very work that the Father has given me to finish, and
> which I am doing, testifies that the Father has sent me'
> (John 5:36; see also John 3: 17; 14:24).

The teaching of the apostles follows accordingly. The Father is the originator of salvation for sinners (Ephesians 1:3-5). The Father is the one to whom sinners are reconciled through Jesus Christ (2 Corinthians 5:18). In prayer we seek the Father through the mediation of the Son and by the leading of the Holy Spirit (Ephesians 2:18). Even when Jesus returns and receives universal acclamation, the glory is to God the Father (Philippians 2:11), and at the end of time the kingdom is to be handed over to the Father:

> ' ... the end will come, when he hands over the kingdom to
> God the Father... then the Son himself will be made subject
> to him who put everything under him so that God may be all
> in all' (1 Corinthians 15:24–28).

We are indeed to give glory to Jesus Christ, God's Son, in the light of his being both God and man, and because he is the only Saviour by his sacrificial death, his rising from the dead and his continuing intercession for us. But we will fail to glorify the Son if we do not follow his example and obey his instruction to glorify the Father. We are also to give glory to the Holy Spirit, but we fail to do so in a biblical manner if we do not follow him as the one who alone can and does reveal the Father to us and give us the spiritual energy without which we will not and cannot come to the Father.

It is not wrong for us to sing the praises of our Lord Jesus Christ, the eternal Son of God and offer prayers to him. Likewise we may properly worship the Holy Spirit, thanking him for his loving ministry and seeking his enabling in our life and service. But if we follow Scripture our prayers, praises and petitions will be directed first of all to the Father who is the

> 'one God and Father of all, who is over all and through all and in all' (Ephesians 4:6; see also Philippians 4:20).

Dr. D. Martyn Lloyd Jones in his sermon on Ephesians 1:15-17 comments:

> '... I have sometimes gained the impression that many Christians seem to think that the hallmark of spirituality is to pray to the Lord Jesus Christ. But when we turn to the Scriptures we discover that that is not really so, and that, as here, prayers are normally offered to the Father. The Lord Jesus Christ is the mediator, not the end; he is the One who brings us to the Father. We go to the Father by him; he is the great High Priest; he is our representative. Normally we do not pray to him, but to the Father, in the name of the Lord Jesus Christ... I have sometimes thought that perhaps the greatest danger confronting evangelicals at the present time is (and I speak with reverence) so to emphasise the Person of the Son as to forget the Father. We fail to realise that the Son came to glorify the Father and to bring us to him'.
> (*God's Ultimate Purpose:* Lloyd Jones, Banner of Truth)

So we are right to spend time considering God as our Father and we can be sure this will be a great help in our spiritual experience. But will this result in our worship being heavy and sombre? No! In our public and private worship we should strive to be truly Trinitarian, giving honour to the Father, the Son and the Holy Spirit. When we do this, observing the emphases in Scripture, our worship will be reverent, warm, loving, joyful and exuberant. We must develop this theme a little further.

5.
Our Father's praise

The more we discover about God the greater will be our excitement. If we are not moved to joyful praise when we read about our heavenly Father in the Scriptures, we surely have not understood how great he really is. It is impossible for anyone who has the slightest notion of what God is like to remain cold and indifferent or fail to adore him.

Wholehearted praise

The apostle Paul says that we should be united with others in worship:

> 'so that with one heart and mouth you may glorify the God and Father of our Lord Jesus Christ' (Romans 15:6).

Paul cannot help giving praise to the Father:

> 'To God our Father be glory for ever and ever. Amen' (Philippians 4:20).

The fifth commandment instructs us to give honour to our earthly parents (Exodus 20:12). This reflects our duty to honour our heavenly Father. Indeed, obedience to this command should be, and often is, a kind of preparation for the greater privilege.

We are encouraged in this worship by Jesus Christ himself who told a Samaritan woman:

> '... a time is coming and has now come when the true worshippers will worship the Father in Spirit and truth, for they are the kind of worshippers that the Father seeks' (John 4:23).

True worship of the Father will adore him as almighty, holy, righteous and just, and also as gracious, compassionate, tender and merciful. What more do we need to excite our praise and exultation? Think, for example of:

> My God, how wonderful Thou art! Thy Majesty how bright!
> How beautiful thy mercy-seat, in depths of burning light!
> How wonderful, how beautiful, the sight of thee must be,
> Thine endless wisdom, boundless power and awful purity!
> (Frederick W. Faber)

> Father-like he tends and spares us;
> Well our feeble frame he knows;
> In his hands he gently bears us,
> Rescues us from all our foes;
> Praise him! Praise him!
> Widely as his mercy flows.
> (Henry F. Lyte)

Shame on us that we can sing such words with our minds wandering and without the involvement of our whole being!

Nothing can stimulate praise to our Father and joy in him more than the realisation that 'God so loved the world that he gave his one and only Son' (John 3:16). Salvation originated with the Father, he did not spare his Son but 'gave him up for us all' (Romans 8:32). Not only so, he gives the Holy Spirit to those who ask him (Luke 11:13). No wonder Paul was led to exclaim:

> 'Praise be to the God and Father of our Lord Jesus Christ who has blessed us in the heavenly realms with every spiritual blessing in Christ. For he chose us in him before the creation of the world to be holy and blameless in his sight' (Ephesians 1:3-4).

> '... joyfully giving thanks to the Father, who has qualified you to share in the inheritance of the saints in the kingdom of light. For he has rescued us from the dominion of darkness and brought us into the kingdom of the Son he loves' (Colossians 1:11-13).

When a church sees these things clearly there is no lack of gospel preaching nor of spiritual excitement and fervour in our worship. We feel something of the awe, wonder, sense of privilege and joy of the psalmist when he exclaimed:

'This God is our God, for ever and ever' (Psalm 48:14)

and,

'Shout with joy to God, all the earth! Sing the glory of his name; make his praise glorious! Say to God, "How awesome are your deeds! So great is your power that your enemies cringe before you' (Psalm 66:1-3).

A girl known to me had a problem because she could worship Jesus and be thankful for the Holy Spirit but she could not love God the Father. The reason was that she had been abused by her natural father. There are all too many people with that understandable difficulty. The answer is this; we would not have either Jesus Christ or the Holy Spirit if our heavenly Father had not loved us enough to give them to us.

We should not allow ourselves to be put into a straight jacket in our worship. Indeed, when we worship God as our Father we should enjoy the liberty of being his children. The Father is not honoured by shapeless, mindless worship (so-called), but we should feel free to give ourselves to full-throated singing and spontaneous response to what we hear in appreciative laughter and fervent amens and hallelulias.

The Father in evangelism

Praise and worship take many forms and one of them is the preaching of the gospel and telling others the great things God has done for our salvation. When we see evangelism in this light it has a new joy and fullness.

The Fatherhood of God also gives substance and direction to our evangelism. Many people feel no need of the gospel because they do not realise they have sinned against God, nor appreciate the awesome nature of God's judgement. For this reason we need to begin our evangelism more often with God as the judge of all men and as the one to whom we must be reconciled.

Jesus spoke of salvation as coming to the Father —

> '... I am the way and the truth and the life. No one comes to the Father except through me' (John 14:6).

And he put these words into the mouth of the younger son in his parable:

> 'I will set out and go back to my father and say to him: Father I have sinned...' (Luke 15:18).

At Athens Paul had been speaking to people about Jesus and the resurrection (Acts I7:18), but when he was challenged to make a statement about the Christian faith to people who were totally ignorant of the Scriptures he began with God the Creator of all things (Acts 17:22-24). Ours is a similar generation; there is:

> '... a scandalous lack of knowledge and ignorance about Jesus Christ... generations are growing up who have never heard of Jesus Christ and who believe the word god is an expletive'.
> (Canon Colin Semper, reported in Daily Telegraph, 22nd February 1994).

We need increasingly to take Paul in Athens as our pattern. We need joyfully to proclaim forgiveness in Jesus Christ in the context of a God who has revealed himself and has intervened into human history. We can give him no greater praise. The result will be praise to the Father for the blessings he gives such as pardon for our sins, peace and joy, and more besides. The ultimate purpose of the gospel is to put us right with God as our judge, so that we can then live with him as our heavenly Father; a relationship that grows in meaning and is unhindered by death.

Praise and assurance

We have already thought about Christian assurance in chapter 3; now we can add that a practical effect of honouring the Father is the strengthening it gives to our assurance of salvation. This in turn will stimulate our worship. All believers should be assured of God's love for them by the witness of the Holy Spirit in their hearts (Romans 8:16). The confidence of every Christian should be rooted in the words of the Lord Jesus,

> 'My sheep listen to my voice; I know them, and they follow me. I give them eternal life and they shall never perish; no one can snatch them out of my hand' (John 10:27-28).

But we should notice that our Lord did not leave the matter there; he went on to say:

> 'My Father, who has given them to me, is greater than all, no one can snatch them out of my Father's hand' (v.29).

And in his prayer to the Father in John 17, Jesus spoke frequently of 'those whom you gave me' (vv. 2, 6, 9, and 24). All this reminds us that ultimately our security is embedded in eternity past when the Father chose us in Christ:

> '... God's elect...who have been chosen according to the foreknowledge of God the Father...' (1 Peter 1:1-2).

This is the way to a robust Christian life, personally satisfying and strong enough to help those who are in danger of losing the joy of salvation. Such assurance must result in praise, worship and thanksgiving, and lead us on to the enjoyment of what it means to be children of God.

> 'Now to the King eternal, immortal, invisible, the only God, be honour and glory for ever and ever, Amen' (1 Timothy 1:17).

> Praise my soul the King of Heaven
> To his feet thy tribute bring
> Ransomed, healed, restored, forgiven
> Who like thee his praise should sing
> Praise him! Praise him!
> Praise the everlasting King.
> (Henry F Lyte).

6.
Our Father made everything

When little children feel threatened they are prone to say to their persecutors 'my Dad's bigger than your Dad'. Where they hardly know who their father is or which of the men around them is Daddy, confidence in this resource of strength and protection is whittled away. So it is when we acknowledge no God or make ourselves dependent on many gods such as material things or idols of the entertainment world — we have no spiritual resources to call on. Christians are not to be childish in the sense of being fickle or having temper tantrums, but we are to be childlike in humility and simple trust. None of us should be so pompous that we cannot say reverently and confidently to every enemy of our souls, 'My Father made everything, he's bigger than you, so you can't hurt me'.

Creator of the world

The Bible speaks of God the Father as the Creator of the world. It is true that both the Son (John 1:1-4; Colossians 1:15-16) and the Holy Spirit (Genesis 1:1-2; Job 33:4; Psalm 104:27–30) were involved in the creation, but as with everything else the universe was planned by the Father and brought into being at his command.

> 'By the word of the LORD were the heavens made, their starry host by the breath of his mouth. He gathers the waters of the sea into jars; he puts the deep into storehouses. Let all the earth fear the LORD; let all the people of the world revere him. For he spoke, and it came to be; he commanded, and it stood firm' (Psalm 33:6-9).

In Psalm 90:1-2 we read:

> 'Lord you have been our dwelling place throughout all generations. Before the mountains were born or you brought forth the earth and the world, from everlasting to everlasting you are God.'

The words used here 'born' and 'brought forth' give us the remarkable illustration of God giving birth to the creation. This must not be taken literally, but the thought harmonises with the idea of God the Father as the originator of all things.

The key passage in the New Testament is 1 Corinthians 8:4-6:

> '... We know that an idol is nothing at all in the world and that there is no God but one. For even if there are so-called gods, whether in heaven or on earth (as indeed there are many "gods" and many "lords"), yet for us there is but one God, the Father, from whom all things came and for whom we live...'

The contrast in this passage between idols and God is tremendously important for our understanding and for our spiritual experience in at least three ways.

The Father is a person

The first is the clear indication that our God is a person, 'he' not 'it'. It is true that in another place Paul seems to speak of idols as though they were personal beings when he says 'The sacrifices of pagans are offered to demons' (1 Corinthians 10:20), but the idols themselves to which those sacrifices were offered were either man-made objects or parts of creation such as the sun or mountains or animals. The common factor was that these idols could not think or plan or speak or move on their own initiative to help or to encourage anyone.

> 'Our God is in heaven; he does whatever pleases him. But their idols are silver and gold, made by the hands of men.

They have mouths, but cannot speak, eyes, but they cannot
see; they have ears, but cannot hear, noses, but they cannot
smell; they have hands, but cannot feel, feet, but they cannot
walk; nor can they utter a sound with their throats. Those
who make them will be like them, and so will all who trust
in them' (Psalm 115:3-8).

Our Father God is by definition a person. This distinguishes him
from such impersonal ideas as luck or fate. Luck has no ability to
plan and results in chaos not beauty. Fate is blind, dictating everything without purpose, without feeling. The 'force' of science
fiction has some degree of personality but offers no intimate
personal relationship to us. But when we know the Creator is God
the Father and that he is 'our Father in heaven' (Matthew 6:9) we are
liberated from uncertainty, a sense of isolation and from frustration
because everything has meaning, purpose and direction.

The Father is unlimited

Secondly, the fact that our Father is the Creator of all things means
he has infinite wisdom, power and goodness (Acts 14:14–17;
Romans 1:18-20). A Christian, weakened by the buffetings of the
world, the flesh and the devil, can look up to the night sky, or at the
exquisite shape of a rose, or drink in the breathtaking grandeur of a
mountain range and say, 'My Father made that'. This is what the
Scriptures encourage us to do:

'Lift your eyes and look to the heavens. Who created all
these? He who brings out the starry host one by one, and
calls them each by name. Because of his great power and
mighty strength not one of them is missing. Why do you say,
O Jacob, and complain, O Israel, 'My way is hidden from the
LORD; my cause is disregarded by my God?' Do you not
know? Have you not heard? The LORD is the everlasting
God, the Creator of the ends of the earth. He will not grow
tired or weary, and his understanding no-one can fathom'
(Isaiah 40:26-28).

In times of weakness we can say to ourselves, 'My Father must be very wise, very good and very strong' and this gives us new heart.

The Father is separate from his creation

The third very important thing is this, God the Father, the Creator of all things, is separate from his creation. He is transcendent, which means that he is apart from all things and above all things. This is important because there is a growing belief in the idea that God is nature and nature is God. This is called Pantheism — (pan = all things, theism = to do with god, thus, 'god is all things'). The idea can extend to people; New Age teachers tell us to look inside ourselves and we will find god. This kind of thing can be found in some eastern religions. The tragedy with these ideas is that God is identified with a fallen world, with all its frustration (Romans 8:20), catastrophes, agony and shame. I cannot think why the idea that we are gods is regarded as 'New Age' thinking. There is nothing new about it, people have had dreams (or nightmares) like it throughout history. What hope is there if our lives are in our hands; all human history should teach us the sheer folly in trusting in humankind.

'It is better to take refuge in the LORD than to trust in man.
It is better to take refuge in the LORD than to trust in princes'
(Psalm 118:8-9).

Thank God we can look outside ourselves to the all-powerful, all-wise Creator and sustainer of all things — our Father in heaven. We can trust him, talk to him and listen to him. He is the:

Centre and soul of every sphere,
Yet to each loving heart, how near.
(Oliver Wendell Holmes)

But when we say that God is transcendent, above all things, we do not mean that he is unconcerned about the world and its sufferings — far from it. There is no doubt that God shares the pain of his people when they suffer, even when that suffering is part of his chastening of them. As the prophet Isaiah tells us:

'In all their distress he too was distressed' (lsaiah 63:9).

And one of the greatest statements about God in the whole of Scripture is 'God is Love' (1 John 4:8,16); can we think of love that has no feeling of pity or pain in the face of the misery and anguish of others? Such love would be a complete sham. It is a true saying:

> There is no place where earth's sorrows are more felt than
> up in heaven. (Frederick. F. Faber)

God is apart from his world, he is not a victim of its troubles but rather is controlling all things toward the resolving of the world's problems and releasing it from all the effects of sin. He intervenes in the course of creation and human history. If God were part of his world, he would be powerless and no help to us at all; we would be limited by our own resources. But as it is, he is in control:

> He reigns! Ye saints, exalt your strains;
> Your God is King, your Father reigns.
> (Josiah Condor)

Make no mistake; our God is a person with whom we can relate, he is unlimited in wisdom and strength we can rely on and he is in control of all that happens, giving us confidence and hope.

7.
Our Father saves

The three persons of the Trinity — Father, Son and Holy Spirit, are at one in the plan and work of our salvation from sin and its consequences. It is also true that because Jesus Christ actually died in our place and rose again, he is the one we rightly speak of as the Saviour.

> 'Here is a trustworthy saying that deserves full acceptance: Christ Jesus came into the world to save sinners...'
> (1 Timothy 1:15).

> 'Grace and peace from God the Father and Christ Jesus our Saviour' (Titus 1:4).

And yet we may also delight in the fact that our Father saves. Our attention is frequently drawn to this in the Scriptures, for example Mary began her song of worship:

> 'My soul glorifies the Lord, and my spirit rejoices in God my saviour' (Luke 1:46-47).

The apostle Paul began his comprehensive explanation of salvation in his letter to the Romans by describing it as 'the gospel of God' (Romans 1:1), and in other letters he often calls God 'our Saviour' (1 Timothy 1:1; 2:3; Titus 1:3). This does not mean that the Father was born at Bethlehem nor that he died on the cross, but it does mean that the Father planned our salvation, ensured that the plan was put into operation and that he is determined to bring it to a successful conclusion. Commenting on Romans 1:1 Dr. Lloyd Jones says:

> '... the teaching of the Scripture is... that salvation is the work of the three persons in the blessed Holy Trinity. It is primarily that of the Father — the gospel of God concerning

his Son. The Father first! It is the Father's plan; it is the Father's purpose; it is the Father who initiates it; it is the Father who gave the first promise concerning it to Adam and Eve in the garden of Eden, and, Oh! we must be clear about this. We must not go on to consider what the Son has done, what the Holy Spirit has done and still does, until we are absolutely clear about the primacy of the Father, and the origin of it all in the Father himself. Is it not amazing that we can ever forget it? If there is one verse in the Bible that everybody knows it is John 3:16 and John 3:16 says this: 'God so loved the world that he gave (God the Father gave) his only begotten Son...'. You notice the order. It is God who has done it. It is God who has initiated it all. He is the promoter, as it were, and the prompter of it all — God the Father.'
(*The Gospel of God*. Banner of Truth)

The danger of limiting the work of salvation to Jesus Christ is seen when some people fall into the temptation of thinking that Jesus gave his life to persuade God to love us and forgive us. It is not easy for us to love, trust and praise the Father if we have lingering thoughts that he was reluctant to provide for our salvation. So let us develop this theme a little further to give us reason for whole-hearted love and devotion to our heavenly Father.

The Old Testament ascribes the origins of salvation to the Father:

'Yet, O LORD, you are our Father. We are the clay, you are the potter; we are all the work of your hand' (Isaiah 64:8).

Isaiah also calls the Father the Redeemer of his people:

'... you are our Father, though Abraham does not know us or Israel acknowledge us, you O LORD are our Father, our Redeemer from of old is your name' (Isaiah 63:16).

God redeemed his people when he delivered them from Egyptian slavery, and again when he restored them to their land from captivity in Babylon. In the Old Testament a redeemer was the protector of a family and its property, so God as the Father of Israel undertook all the obligations involved in their safety and security. He was in this sense their Saviour. He said,

> '... there is no God apart from me, a righteous God and a Saviour; there is none but me' (Isaiah 45:21).

These historical events are pictures of what God does for us in the Lord Jesus Christ. So we can apply to ourselves the words that follow in Isaiah;

> 'Turn to me, and be saved, all you ends of the earth; for I am God and there is no other' (Isaiah 45:22).

Everlasting love

In Jeremiah 31:3 God assured his people 'I have loved you with an everlasting love; I have drawn you with loving-kindness'. In the New Testament this whole idea is expanded. We see the Father originating salvation before the world began and guaranteeing its completion in eternal glory. Everything began with the foreknowledge of God:

> 'For those God foreknew he also predestined to be conformed to the likeness of his Son, that he might be the firstborn among many brothers' (Romans 8:29).

The idea of foreknowledge can appear to be rather forbidding, but it is more thrilling than the word at first suggests. It certainly includes God knowing in advance all that is going to happen, but the main thought is love. In biblical terms 'knowledge' often means an intimate love relationship. So we can now see that our salvation began in eternity when the Father set his love upon us and determined to rescue us from our hopeless plight.

Clearly this is far removed from any kind of reluctance on the part of the Father to forgive us. The truth is that the Father's love is the reason and motivation for the sending of Jesus into the world (John 3:16). Jesus came to do the Father's will (John 4:34; Matthew 26:39). Jesus spoke about 'those whom the Father has given me' (John 6:37) and he used the same expression more than once in his prayer to the Father recorded in John 17 (see verses 4,7). This is an aspect of our salvation most of us should relish more than we do. We were not given to Jesus Christ when we believed — the Father gave us to his Son before he came, before we sinned, before Adam fell, before the world began. He loved us then; he was our Saviour then.

The Father sent his Son

At the moment the Father's wisdom determined, he sent his Son into the world:

> ' When the time had fully come, God sent his Son...'
> (Galatians 4:4)

> '... we have seen and testify that the Father has sent his Son
> to be the Saviour of the world' (1 John 4:14).

We must not read 'The Father has sent his Son' in a matter-of-fact kind of way. If we do we will fail to see 'the heart of God revealed' in all that was involved in the sending. Perhaps if we trudge step by step up Mount Moriah with Abraham and his only son Isaac, we will begin to feel the Father's pulse. God had said to Abraham, 'Take your son, your only son Isaac, whom you love. .. sacrifice him' (Genesis 22:2). We can hear Isaac saying, 'The fire and wood are here but where is the lamb for the burnt offering?' and the resolute Abraham saying, 'God himself will provide the lamb for the burnt offering, my son' (Genesis 22:7-8). Abraham was willing to sacrifice his only son whom he loved. Our imagination struggles to feel the agony and foreboding as we see the knife raised to kill his beloved son Isaac for a sacrifice.

The love of a father for his son, especially if it is his only son, is very deep indeed, and God says that it illustrates his love for his people. When he wanted to explain his care for his people and his delight in them he said through the prophet Malachi:

> '... I will spare them, just as in compassion a man spares his
> son who serves him' (Malachi 3:17).

But for our salvation, God did not spare his only Son, for Paul tells us that God:

> '...did not spare his own Son, but gave him up for us all' (Romans 8:32).

In fact, God treated the Son he loved from all eternity and who pleased him always, in the same way that he treated the angels who sinned and for whom there is no salvation.

> '... God did not spare angels when they sinned, but sent them to hell, putting them into gloomy dungeons to be held for judgement' (2 Peter 2:4).

In sheer wonder we can only ask 'Did my Father really go the length of giving his Son up to such a fate as that for me?' And our faith replies, 'Yes, my Father loved me as much as that'. He sent his Son to bear the full unmitigated judgement on my sin out of undeserved, uncalled-for love and pity. Do not misunderstand this. We are concentrating on the love of God the Father, but let us remember that God is one. This means that the Son was not a reluctant victim of a plan imposed on him, but partner in that plan and that he willingly played his part. Jesus himself put this straight!

> 'The reason my Father loves me is that I lay down my life — only to take it up again. No-one takes it from me, but I lay it down of my own accord. I have authority to lay it down and authority to take it up again. This command I received from my Father' (John 10:17-18).

The Father sends his Spirit

There is yet more to follow in the saving work of our heavenly Father. He planned our salvation, he loved us before time, he chose us in the Lord Jesus Christ and sent his Son into the world to bear the punishment of sin for us. And his rescue operation did not stop there, because the Bible also tells us that he 'calls' us:

'... we ought always to thank God for you, brothers loved by
the Lord, because from the beginning God chose you to be
saved through the sanctifying work of the Spirit and through
belief in the truth. He called you to this through our gospel...' (2 Thessalonians 2:13-14).

'... those he predestined he also called, those he called he
also justified...' (Romans 8:30).

What is this 'calling' ? It means that just as the Father sent the Son
to die for us, so he sends the Holy Spirit to enlighten us and give us
eternal life. This is the way he summons us out of darkness into light,
and out of death into life.

And then there is our Father's welcome. When the Spirit has
awakened us to our need and shown us the way of salvation we turn
to our Father as the lost son did in the Lord's story:

'...he got up and went to his father. But while he was still a
long way off, his father saw him and was filled with
compassion for him; he ran to his son, threw his arms around
him and kissed him' (Luke 15:20).

Whenever the reality and enormity of our sin lays us low, we can
share the heavy repentant steps of that boy and then the sheer joy of
the Father's welcome.

Enabling grace

But even that does not complete the story of the Father as our
Saviour. From the moment he welcomes us to the moment he
receives us into glory he sustains us in our spiritual experience. It is
this that Paul underlines in the introduction to many of his letters.
For example, 'Grace and peace to you from God our Father...'
(Romans 1:7; see also Galatians 1:3; Ephesians 1:2; Phillipians 1:2;
Colossians 1:2). Very often commentators make these words apply
to our initial salvation by grace, taking us back to the 'call' we have
just thought about, but Paul is writing to people who are already
called and saved by grace, and now he is assuring them of the

continuation of that grace in enabling them to persevere to the end. Grace is a tremendous concept. It embraces all the wisdom of the Father, his love and his power made available through the Lord Jesus Christ to all his children. Enabling grace is the great glory of the Christian life that puts it into a different bracket from every other kind of life.

Our Father gives us more and more of his Spirit's help, and Jesus assures us that if we ask for the Spirit to fill us the Father will grant that request:

> 'Which of you fathers, if your son asks for a fish, will give him a snake instead? Or if he asks for an egg, will give him a scorpion? If you then, though you are evil, know how to give good gifts to your children, how much more will your Father in heaven give the Holy Spirit to those who ask him!' (Luke 11:11-13).

We are particularly vulnerable to temptation when we first become children of God. We are babes, little ones, and Jesus tells us that our Father has a host of angels watching over us because he is not willing that any of us should be lost (Matthew 18:10-14). This is at least one reason why we survive the early days of the Christian life, though we do not realise it at the time!

The Father, then, is our Saviour. He has loved us from eternity, he sent his Son to die for us and his Spirit to transform us and enable us to go on in the Christian life to the end of our life on earth. So, let us join with Mary, the mother of Jesus in words we have already quoted:

> 'My spirit rejoices in God my Saviour'.

8.
Our Father's embrace

It is all too easy for us to settle for a superficial view of the Christian life and a sub-standard spiritual experience. For many believers the Christian life is all right so far as it goes, but little more.

So far so good

For instance some people never get beyond trying to follow the example of Jesus Christ. They trust him as their Saviour and seek the help of the Holy Spirit in modelling their lives on the Lord. This is good, and the world would be a better place if all Christians took this way of life seriously. So far, so good.

Closely related to these are believers whose whole understanding of the Christian life is in terms of strict obedience to the Scriptures. They diligently examine every part of their lives and all their relationships, and constantly reform themselves according to fresh light they receive on the requirements of God's Word. Who would want to criticise such honourable principles? And yet we have to say that if this is as far as their Christianity goes, it falls far short of the vibrant experience the Lord intends for us; it is all right as far as it goes, but we need to remember that we are 'not under law but under grace' (Romans 6:14-15).

Then there are people whose Christianity is church-life centred. Their life is filled with a routine of meetings; they can always be relied on to be at all the gatherings of the church. They are a joy to the hearts of the elders. Often such folk are also the workers, because 'somebody has to do the work you know!' They are always willing to take on more, 'busy people have the most time, you know!' These are the people to be relied on not to resign when the going is tough. We all know just how valuable such people are. Let us not say a single word that robs a church of one worker like that, but it is dreadfully possible for such a person to be spiritually impoverished; this may be another case of so far, so good. The Christian life is not a routine, it is a relationship.

Our lives can even be centred around spiritual gifts in an unhealthy way. Some sincere believers are so concerned to possess and exercise spiritual gifts as to give the impression that this is their idea of the highest pinnacle of Christian experience. Well, the apostle Paul wrote, 'eagerly desire the greater gifts' (1 Corinthians 12:31), so these friends cannot be entirely wrong. And yet I believe it is sadly possible even for these people to fall short of the best that God has for them.

We can be the most estimable of Christians in terms of conduct, loyalty, and the exercise of spiritual gifts, and yet not enjoy the full blessing of God as our heavenly Father. Let us illustrate this from ordinary family life. Too often, for many of us, the home is merely a place where we work and exercise responsibilities; perhaps it is even just a lodging. But we are supposed to have a happy family life, which means enjoying each other as parents and children, brothers and sisters. In the same way we may call God our Father in our prayers and trust his care for us in the ordinary experiences of life, yet still not have a true spiritual family relationship. Only as we enter more completely into that relationship do we really discover what the Christian life is meant to be like, indeed, what a Christian is, namely, someone who enjoys the Father's embrace.

New Testament believers

The apostle Paul draws a distinction between an Old Testament and a New Testament experience:

> '... the heir is a child ... subject to guardians and trustees until the time set by his father. So also, when we were children, we were in slavery under the basic principles of the world. But when the time had fully come, God sent his Son, born of a woman, born under law, to redeem those under the law that we might receive the full rights of sons. Because you are sons, God has sent the Spirit of his Son into our hearts, the Spirit who calls out 'Abba, Father'. So you are no longer a slave but a son; and since you are a son God has made you also an heir' (Galatians 4:1-7).

Here Paul likens believers in the Old Testament to children who are heirs of the family riches but as yet are not old enough, according to the law, to enter into their heritage. Until they do they are under discipline and their liberty is curtailed. In the same way it is possible for us to live as though the Holy Spirit had not been given. For some people who profess to be Christians the Christian life is one of mechanical obedience, rather like the older son in the Lord's parable (Luke 15:28-32).

New Testament believers are sons in a more complete sense than was possible to those in the Old Testament. Despite this, some live as though having trusted Christ, they still have to do something to placate God instead of realising that they are at liberty to run into his forgiving and welcoming arms. We sometimes treat God as if we need to make an appointment to see him, put on special clothes, and behave according to a prescribed etiquette. But we need to realise that we have freedom of access to our heavenly Father at all times. True, he is King of Kings and Lord of Lords (Revelation 19:16) but we are princes; we not only have free access into his presence, but it is our great privilege to live with him all the time, as Paul says:

> ' ... you did not receive a spirit that makes you a slave again to fear, but you received the Spirit of sonship. And by him we cry, "Abba Father"' (Romans 8:15).

An earthly ruler may need to exclude his child from his presence at times when he is occupied with matters of state, but there is never a moment when we may not see the face of our Father in heaven, we can enjoy his smile all the time without a split-second break. This is the fullness of the Christian experience. The Psalmist could say:

> 'You have made known to me the path of life, you will fill me with joy in your presence, with eternal pleasures at your right hand' (Psalm 16:11).

Those who have received the Spirit of sonship can most certainly understand what he means and even more so.

Not long before Jesus Christ died he said to his disciples,

> 'Though I have been speaking figuratively, a time is coming when I will no longer use this kind of language but will tell

you plainly about my Father. In that day you will ask in my name. I am not saying that I will ask the Father on your behalf. No, the Father himself loves you...' (John 16:25-27).

At first sight this may seem to contradict other Scriptures that tell us that Jesus is in the Father's presence and is always praying for us (Romans 8:34; Hebrews 7:23-25). But our Lord is not saying that these prayers will come to an end, rather he is underlining the fact that his intercession does not mean that there is a barrier between us and our Father. These words of Jesus mean that he does not have to pray for us to persuade the Father to love us, receive us and hear our prayers. The Father himself loves us; Jesus is not a barrier between us, but the means of our direct access to the ear and heart of the Father.

What is a Christian?

Knowing God as our Father is in a sense a definition of a Christian. We can see this in the words of Jesus:

'... I am the way, and the truth and the life. No one comes to the Father except through me' (John 14:6.:

There are all kinds of ways in which we may quite properly describe what it means to be a Christian. We delight in reconciliation to God, in Jesus Christ as our Lord and Saviour and in the life changing power of the Holy Spirit. And then we also understand that a Christian is someone who has eternal life; but what is eternal life? Our Lord himself gave us the answer:

'... Father ... this is eternal life that they may know you...' (John 17:1,3).

As we have seen in chapter 7, when the Bible speaks of knowledge it includes the idea of a intimate loving relationship. So that eternal life is not only knowing about God but living in a very close relationship with him. Eternal life is an endless experience of joyful, trusting, praising, and soul-satisfying fellowship with the most high God — our heavenly Father. This is the complete destruction of any idea that the Christian life is a series of services, meetings and quiet times. These things are good in themselves but all too many of us have a staccato, on/off relationship with God which is less than satisfying. We need to explore the privilege now open to us as children of God to realise his fatherly presence, strength, wisdom love and joy as a continuous unbroken experience embracing our whole life.

We are also able to grow in this knowledge. Many of the pictures of the Christian life in Scripture imply growth; branches of a vine bearing fruit (John 15:1-18) a body that matures (Ephesians 4:15-16), and a baby who becomes bigger and stronger (1 Peter 2:2).

An earthly father is very distressed if his child is stunted, failing to grow physically. In the same way our heavenly Father looks for his children to grow spiritually:

> 'Like new born babies, crave pure spiritual milk, so that you may grow up in your salvation' (1 Peter 2:2).

> '... your faith is growing more and more, and the love every one of you has for each other is increasing' (2 Thessalonians 1:3).

> '... grow in grace and knowledge of our Lord and Saviour Jesus Christ...' (2 Peter 3:18).

> '... bearing fruit in every good work, growing in the knowledge of God...' (Colossians 1:10).

As natural children we grow up, and in the process we grow in the knowledge of our parents — their way of thinking, their principles and ambitions. The Christian life should likewise be one of growth in the knowledge of our heavenly Father and in our love for him, our appreciation of his mind, his desires and his designs for us and for his world. There can be a kind of progression in some people's religious experience worked out in the stages of their attitude to God. They begin with 'O God' signifying their recognition that God has the right to direct their lives and they should obey him. But their entry into a love relationship with God is signalled by their beginning to speak to God as 'my Father' not merely using the words but feeling the depth of their meaning.

The hesitation of people to call God 'Father' reflects the sheer wonder of what Jesus Christ has made possible. Human reason would never have thought of such a thing or have worked out how it would be possible for sinful people to love God, transcendent and unapproachably holy, as their caring Father. Perhaps the wonder of all this comes home to us when we hear the story of how some-one who has been a Muslim has struggled to pluck up the courage even to think of a love relationship with God. Such people can be consumed with fear that the wrath of the Almighty will strike them dead if they dare to call God 'Father'. But this is the authentic Christian message and experience — it is the glory of our faith.

We must not stop trying to obey the Lord as he makes his will known to us in the Scriptures. We must go on serving him in the fellowship of the church and seeking to develop the gifts and talents he has given us. But these are not to be an end in themselves, rather they should be means in and through which our Father draws us on to the enjoyment of himself — his embrace.

9.
Our Father's perfect Son

Before we go any further into our relationship with our heavenly Father, let us look at the one and only perfect example we have been given. When God wanted to show us what his Fatherhood would mean for him and for us, he sent his Son Jesus Christ into the world. He was God's Son in a unique way as the second person of the Trinity, and that is totally outside of our range. As Jesus himself said,

> '... No-one knows the Son except the Father, and no-one knows the Father except the Son and those to whom the Son chooses to reveal him' (Matthew 11:27).

The Jews were right when they understood Jesus calling God his Father to mean that he was claiming to be equal with God (John 5:17-18). Jesus himself confirmed this when he said 'I and the Father are one' (John 10:30); this meant more than that they were united in their aims, though that was true. Our Lord was saying that he is God in exactly the same sense that the Father is God — they were united in their Godhead.

His Father and ours

When God sent his Son into the world their relationship was sustained, as we can see from the number of times Jesus spoke to God or about God as his Father — for example:

> 'Whoever acknowledges me before men I will also acknowledge him before my Father in heaven. But whoever disowns me before men, I will disown him before my Father in heaven' (Matthew 10:32-33).

'...I praise you, Father, Lord of heaven and earth, because you have hidden these things from the wise and learned, and revealed them to little children. Yes, Father, for this was your good pleasure' (Matthew 11:25-26 see also Matthew 7:21; 12:50; 15:13; 16:17; 18:10; 19:35; 20:23; 26:39, 42, 53).

As we read the gospels we can see the wonderful relationship of the Father and the Son translated for our sakes into human terms. This is a picture of what the Fatherhood of God can mean to us. Our Lord made a clear distinction between his relationship to the Father and ours, and yet he did not hesitate to draw the parallel. He asked Mary at the empty tomb to tell the disciples:

'I am returning to my Father and your Father' (John 20:17).

He did not say 'Our Father' because that would have meant his disciples were on the same level as himself. And yet in the same breath he assured them that his Father was their Father too.

His Father's love

Jesus used his Father's relationship with himself to illustrate his own love for us. He told his disciples:

'As the Father has loved me, so have I loved you'
(John 15:9).

What could help our understanding of the love of Jesus for us more effectively than these remarkable words? The Father's love for his Son is of the greatest intensity that we could ever imagine, and to realise that this is how Jesus loves us must fill us with unspeakable joy. If our Lord had not spoken like this we would never have dared to think that his love for his people was at such a high level.

But then in his prayer to the Father recorded in John 17 Jesus said something even more remarkable:

'... you sent me and have loved them even as you have loved me'.

'I have made you known to them, and will continue to make
you known in order that the love you have for me may be in
them...' (vv.23,26).

It is almost unbelievable, that the Father loves his children in the
same way that he loves his Son. Again we can only believe this
because Jesus has told us it is so. Think of how God the Father loves
his Son. It is eternal, intimate, constant and never wavering. Here are
things completely outside our comprehension but there are hints in
Scripture that pull aside the curtain just a little. For instance, Jesus
prayed to his Father:

'... you loved me before the creation of the world'
(John 17:24).

and then the apostle John tells us,

'In the beginning was the Word and the Word was with God'
(John 1:1).

The little word 'with' contains the idea of an active relationship, the
closest possible fellowship and delight in each other. Furthermore,
it is in the continuous tense, telling us that this close communion
between the Father and the Son before the world began was never
ending. The sense of this is captured by the translation in the
Authorised Version:

'No man hath seen God at any time; the only begotten Son,
which is in the bosom of the Father, he hath declared him'
(John 1:18; see also 1 John 1:2).

Nothing could convince us that our Father loves us to such an
unbelievable extent than the assurance we have from our Lord
himself.

So dear, so very dear to God,
More dear I cannot be;
The love wherewith he loves the Son —
Such is his love to me.
(Catesby Paget)

His Father's commission

After his resurrection Jesus told his disciples

'As the Father has sent me I am sending you' (John 20:21).

Here again we see the unique relationship between the Father and the Son as a pattern for us. We are sent into the world just as surely as Jesus was sent. If ever we are tempted to doubt the Lord's intention that we should spread the gospel far and wide, those words must surely put an end to such thoughts. His commission to us is as serious and as indispensable as the mission of Christ when he came into the world. This lifts every form of witnessing and evangelising to the highest possible level of importance.

The perfect Son

Just as the gospels show us God's perfect Fatherhood they also show us Jesus Christ as the perfect Son. Jesus was always concerned for the honour of his Father and the advance of his kingdom. Even at the age of twelve Jesus was totally committed to the Father's work when he reasoned with his parents;

'Didn't you know I had to be in my Father's house?'
(Luke 2:49).

We are not surprised that later during his short ministry Jesus twice purged the temple of dishonest trading that disgraced and disgusted his Father (John 2:13-17; Matthew 21:12-16). At all times Jesus obeyed his Father. He was able to say 'I always do what pleases him' (John 8:29), and he went so far as to say:

'The reason my Father loves me is that I lay down my life
— only to take it up again. No one takes it from me, but I lay
it down of my own accord. I have authority to lay it down
and authority to take it up again. This command I received
from my Father' (John 10:17-18).

Jesus never lost touch with his Father; he was always speaking to him in prayer. At his baptism (Luke 3:21), when he chose his apostles (Luke 6:12-16), in preparation for his crucifixion (Matthew 26:36) and on numerous other occasions (Matthew 14:23; Luke 9:29; 11:1) we find him in prayer. Sometimes he prayed all night, and we might wish that we could have listened to him then. Perhaps we are given a glimpse of his fellowship with his Father in John 17, which is the only extended record we have of our Lord in prayer.

At the end, when he had suffered the unspeakable pain of punishment for our sins,

> 'Jesus called out with a loud voice, "Father, into your hands
> I commit my spirit"' (Luke 23:46).

Although his Father's face had been turned from him Jesus did not doubt his Father's love and care.

How wonderful that he should say 'My Father and your Father'! (John 20:17). What the Father was to Jesus, he is also to those who are his children through faith.

Constant care

We see in the life of Jesus Christ the perfect example of how the Father cares. Any reading of the gospels will convince us that the Father never took his eyes off his Son except in that supreme moment when he was 'made sin' for us (2 Corinthians 5:21) so that he cried, 'My God, my God, why have you forsaken me?' (Matthew 27:46).

At all other times the Father and the Son were inseparable; their eternal union was not disturbed in any way by the testing of human experience. Jesus was conscious of continuous fellowship with his Father in such a way that he was able to say:

> '... If I go and prepare a place for you, I will come back and
> take you to be with me that you also may be where I am'
> (John 14:3).

We might have expected him to say 'that you also may be where I will be'; what he does say may appear strange unless we understand that in one sense he never left the Father's presence.

It would seem that for our sakes, the Father demonstrated his watchfulness over his Son on certain specific occasions. He revealed his presence to Jesus at his baptism as we have already seen (Matthew 3:17) and again at his transfiguration (Matthew 17:5). Then almost on the eve of our Lord's arrest, trial and crucifixion, the Father responded to his Son's prayer:

> "'Father, glorify your name!" Then a voice came from heaven "I have glorified it and will glorify it again"'
> (John 12:28-29).

Not only so, but at his arrest Jesus asked his disciples,

> 'Do you think I cannot call on my Father and he will at once put at my disposal more than twelve legions of angels?' (Matthew 26:53).

Notice the words 'at once'. The Father was at his Son's elbow ready to respond immediately to his slightest request.

In all these ways, and many more, the Father was showing us that his care for us will be as constant as his watchfulness over Jesus Christ. The relationship between the Father and Jesus Christ his Son is the perfect pattern, and the wonderful thing is that, as children of God we can follow it, even if at a distance. Jesus' perfect love for his Father and his obedience to his Father's will is our example, while we bask in the warmth of his love and constant care. Let us think about this a little more.

10.
Our Father cares

A lad who was camping with his friends ran out of money; he was certainly not the first nor the last to make that mistake! An urgent appeal to his parents seemed to have fallen on deaf ears. Each morning he was disappointed not to find a letter in the post bringing the needed relief. His friends began to scoff at his discomfort, and at last one of them said to him 'Your Dad has forgotten you!' His reply was immediate and emphatic, 'I don't know what is happening; I don't know why no money has come; I don't know when it will; but I do know this, *my father has not forgotten me.*'

That reply shames many of us who frequently doubt our heavenly Father's care. Many things perplex us and test our faith, and sometimes we are brought almost to despair. In situations like this it is a golden rule that there are some absolutes upon which we must fix our minds and from which we refuse to budge. Abraham demonstrated this in his reasoning with God about the safety of his nephew Lot. For him the absolute was 'Will not the Judge of all the earth do right?' (Genesis 18:25); that was a fixed position and everything else had to fit around it. Habakkuk observed the same rule as we can see from Habakkuk 1:12-13. 'O LORD,... you cannot tolerate wrong.'

All too often, when we are going through a depressing experience we allow our minds to whirl around in questioning circles and we become more and more perplexed. The only way to break out of this confusion is, as I have said, to establish a fixed point from which we refuse to move. An even better way is for those fixed points to be established in advance of problems arising. In every child of God there should be an inbuilt, immovable conviction, 'my Father has not forgotten me'.

Our Father knows

The Bible makes clear to us that after God made everything he did not leave the world to follow its own course apart from him.

> '"To whom will you compare me? Or who is my equal?" says the Holy One. Lift your eyes and look to the heavens. Who created all these? He who brings out the starry host one by one, and calls them each by name. Because of his great power and mighty strength, not one of them is missing' (Isaiah 40:25-26; see also Acts 14:14-18).

God continues to uphold all creation, and to supervise the history of the world so that his purposes will certainly be achieved. Moment by moment the whole world is dependent on God's provision and preservation; we call this his providence.

> 'The LORD is good to all: he has compassion on all he has made' (Psalm 145:9; see also James 1:16).

All this is very comforting, but it is a sad fact that many people never get beyond a confidence in this general care for them. They speak of their 'faith' or of 'faith in God', but they never enjoy the care of God in the context of a personal loving relationship. They think God is too busy with the world in general to be concerned with their individual needs on a one-to-one basis. When Jesus taught his disciples that God was their Father, he did not deny God's universal providence, but he also revealed the Father as great enough to be concerned with the detail of each individual's personal life.

> 'Are not two sparrows sold for a penny? Yet not one of them will fall to the ground apart from the will of your father. And even the very hairs of your head are all numbered. So don't be afraid; you are worth more than many sparrows' (Matthew 10:29-31).

> 'Which of you, if his son asks for bread, will give him a stone? Or if he asks for a fish, will give him a snake? If you, then, though you are evil, know how to give good gifts to your children, how much more will your Father in heaven give good gifts to those who ask him!' (Matthew 7:9-11).

The apostle Paul reflected this truth in the opening of his second letter to the Corinthians:

> 'Praise be to the God and Father of our Lord Jesus Christ, the Father of compassion and God of all comfort, who comforts us in all our troubles' (2 Corinthians 1:3-4).

Perhaps it was the same boy we imagined at the beginning of this chapter who was helping in his father's grocer's shop one day. A passer-by saw him carrying a pile of heavy boxes, he could only just see over the top of them as he struggled to the back of the shop. 'That's too much for you to carry, my boy' said the onlooker; but the reply was simple and direct, *'My father knows how much I can carry'*. And that is the kind of confidence a loving, trusting relationship with our heavenly Father will give us. As Paul wrote,

> 'No temptation has seized you except what is common to man. And God is faithful; he will not let you be tempted beyond what you can bear. But when you are tempted, he will also provide a way out so that you can stand up under it' (1 Corinthians 10:13).

Our whole life is subject to our Father's care. We often speak of the Lord saving souls, but as someone has said, 'souls without bodies are ghosts, and bodies without souls are corpses'. Jesus came to save people, whole people, and our Father cares for us completely.

Do not worry

Many of us are foolish enough to trust our Father for some things and not for others. One person trusts God for his or her eternal destiny but gets into a terrible panic about going into hospital for an operation. Another person is perfectly calm in the face of serious financial problems but worries unceasingly about family matters. This was the kind of mistake the Syrians made when they reckoned the God of the Israelites could only operate on the hills but was powerless in the valleys (1 Kings 20:23). Hills and valleys are both alike to our heavenly Father. We should all tell ourselves every day that there is no part of life our Father does not care about, and that his wisdom love and power are not limited only to some areas of life.

Our physical needs

Probably most Christians have difficulty in trusting the Lord for physical needs. When we become ill or we are handicapped in some way, we worry over whether there will be a cure, how long it will take, and about the long term effects on our family or our employment. This concern is natural — we would be unnatural, not to say stupid, if we did not have such anxieties.

Like many others, Muriel and I lived for 40 years with the knowledge that we would be dependent on the Lord to provide us with a home to live in when we came to retirement. Naturally we often talked about it, prayed about it, and at times we were frankly anxious about it. Wouldn't you be? But at no time did we doubt our heavenly Father would provide — and he did. We gladly joined with many others in telling of our heavenly Father's faithfulness throughout our lives. In marvellous ways, some of which can only be described as miraculous, he met our needs, often anticipating those needs before we realised they existed.

It is sometimes said that because Jesus taught his disciples not to worry (Matthew 6:25-32) it is therefore a sin to be anxious in stressful situations. This may be good logic but it is very poor spiritual counselling. Such reasoning often drives people to yet more worry because they find themselves in a vicious circle in which they worry because they are worried!

The Scripture is much to be preferred:

'As a father has compassion on his children, so the LORD has compassion on those who fear him; for he knows how we are formed, he remembers that we are dust' (Psalm 103:13-14).

There sometimes comes a point when we do slip into unrelieved panic that betrays unbelief and failure to trust our heavenly Father implicitly; this indeed is sinful. But fear can, and often does, live with faith, as the Psalmist put it,

'When I am afraid ... I will not be afraid' (Psalm 56:5-6).

When the disciples were afraid they were going to drown in the storm on the lake, Jesus did not accuse them of sin, but of 'little faith' (Matthew 8:26).

The teaching of our Lord on this subject is clear and plain, the problem is not with his clarity but with our slowness to put his teaching into practice:

> '...do not worry about your life, what you will eat or drink; or about your body, what you will wear. Is not life more important than food, and the body more important than clothes? Look at the birds of the air; they do not sow or reap or store away in barns, and yet your heavenly Father feeds them. Are you not much more valuable than they? Who of you by worrying can add a single hour to his life? And why do you worry about clothes? See how the lilies of the field grow. They do not labour or spin. Yet I tell you that not even Solomon in all his splendour was dressed like one of these. If that is how God clothes the grass of the field, which is here today and tomorrow is thrown into the fire, will he not much more clothe you, O you of little faith? So do not worry, saying, "What shall we eat?" or "What shall we drink?" or "What shall we wear?" For the pagans run after all these things, and your heavenly Father knows that you need them' (Matthew 6:25-32).

There is a tremendous difference between faith in God and belief in fate. The latter is supposed to be a kind of programme built into life that has no purpose, no feeling of pity, and no provision for comfort or sustaining strength. Nor is faith the same as a stoical refusal to be overcome by anxiety or grief. Faith is trust in a heavenly Father who uses every experience for our good (2 Corinthians 4:16-18), has great compassion for us in our suffering and tells us that he is with us to help and sustain us.

Our Father's faithfulness

God is a faithful Father, and his faithfulness is seen yet more clearly when it is contrasted with the unfaithfulness of his people. Again and again in Old Testament days God protested that their treatment of him was not consistent with their being his children, nor did it honour him as their Father.

> 'Is this the way you repay the LORD, O foolish and unwise people? Is he not your Father, your Creator, who made you and formed you?' (Deuteronomy 32:6).

> 'Hear, O heavens! Listen, O earth! For the LORD has spoken; "I reared children and brought them up, but they have rebelled against me"' (Isaiah 1:2; see also Malachi 2:10).

The Lord had the right to expect good conduct and loyalty from the children he had loved and nurtured so faithfully, and he expects the same from us (Ephesians 4:31-5:1). But even though we let him down constantly, as we do, he remains true to his people and never disowns them.

But what has happened when people who trust God as their Father starve to death or are not saved from being tortured to death? Has God failed? Has their faith been faulty? No! A thousand times, No! Centuries before Jesus came with his wonderful teaching about the Fatherhood of God, Job had the right attitude when he said 'Though he slay me, yet will I hope in him' (Job 13:15). Why should a believer in Christ think something is wrong when God decides it is time to release him or her from this sin-ridden world? Why is death so often thought of as a failure on God's part? The writer to the Hebrews had no such problem. For him some people, by faith, were saved from death:

> '...who through faith conquered kingdoms, administered justice, and gained what was promised; who shut the mouths of lions, quenched the fury of the flames, and escaped the edge of the sword; whose weakness was turned to strength, and who became powerful in battle and routed foreign armies. Women received back their dead to life again.'

Others, by faith, died and entered into their eternal inheritance:

> 'Others were tortured and refused to be released, so that they might gain a better resurrection. Some faced jeers and flogging, while still others were chained and put in prison.

They were stoned; they were sawn in two; they were put to
death by the sword' (Hebrews 11:32-38).

Our spiritual needs

All I have said about our Father's care and faithfulness applies just
as much to our spiritual needs. This is important for those to
remember who trust God more easily for material and physical care
than for their spiritual welfare. A key text is the assurance given us
by our Lord himself:

> 'My sheep listen to my voice; I know them and they follow
> me. I give them eternal life, and they shall never perish; no
> one can snatch them out of my hand. My Father, who has
> given them to me, is greater than all; no one can snatch them
> out of my Father's hand' (John 10:27-29).

All our spiritual foes have been robbed of their power to deprive us
of eternal life. Satan is our determined enemy using all kinds of
means to oppose us. He is likened to a wolf that attacks a flock of
sheep (John 10:12) and to a lion pouncing on its prey (1 Peter 5:8)
as he assails us with temptations from the world around us and from
our own sinful nature. He accuses us in the very presence of God
(Zechariah 3:1-2; Romans 8:33). Our assurance that Satan will not
ultimately prevail is based on two things. The first is the superior
power of our heavenly Father, as the song has it: 'He's got the whole
wide world in his hands ... he's got you and me, brother, in his hands'
(author unknown). The second reason for our assurance is that our
Father has loved us since before the world began; it was then he gave
us to the Son. Our Father's care for us did not begin when we first
trusted him, but is eternal.

Bishop Ryle in his expository thoughts on John 10:27-29 quotes
Calvin:

> 'Our salvation is certain because it is in the hand of God. Our
> faith is weak, and we are prone to waver; but God who hath
> taken us under his protection is sufficiently powerful to

scatter with a breath all the power of our adversaries. It is of great importance to turn our eyes to this.'

And Roy Clements quotes a story about the Scottish pastor John Brown:

'He once visited a lady on her death-bed. "Jane," he said, "what would you say if after all that he has done for you, God should let you perish?" The old woman thought for a moment and then she said, ' Well, if he did, he'd lose more than I would, I reckon. For I'd only lose my soul. He'd lose his honour, for he has said 'they shall never perish'
(*Introducing Jesus* Kingsway Publications Ltd)

Let the words clearly echo and re-echo in our minds and hearts — 'our heavenly Father knows, our heavenly Father cares' and there is nothing, absolutely nothing, either physical, material or spiritual that is outside the range of his love. Why do we doubt it?

11.
Our Father's love

We should not be in any doubt that our Father God loves his children because the Scriptures constantly assure us that this is so:

> '...God our Father, who loved us...' (2 Thessalonians 2:16).

> '...those who have been called, who are loved by God the Father...' (Jude 1).

Love for the Lord Jesus Christ, God's Son, automatically brings us into the orbit of our Father's care (John 14:21). Furthermore our Father desires to be with us. Jesus gives us a remarkable picture of those who obey him becoming a home for the Father and the Son to live in:

> '... if anyone loves me, he will obey my teaching. My Father will love him, and we will come to him and make our home with him' (John 14:23).

Our Father is like a mother

It is often said that there is no love like that of a mother. In the continuing debate about the nature of God, it is said that if we always refer to God as 'he' we are guilty of sexual bias and that therefore God should be 'she' as well as 'he'. This is a complete misunderstanding of the Scripture. When we speak of people in masculine terms we are using these terms to include both men and women (Genesis 1:27). To speak of God as 'he' does not infer that he is either male or female, but a person in whose image both men and women are created.

But whenever there is a debate of this kind, some truth we have been in danger of neglecting is often brought to the surface. In this case, undoubtedly we have not drawn as much help as we could have done from the 'feminine' qualities attributed to our God. Perhaps we have not dared to give full weight to the fact that God applies the attributes of motherhood to himself, because we have been afraid of being misunderstood. But we should always be willing to go as far as Scripture takes us in all its teaching and no further.

When we follow Scripture we see that, in contrast to heathen idols that must themselves be carried, God tells us that he is like a mother carrying her children:

> '... you whom I have upheld since you were conceived, and have carried since your birth' (Isaiah 46:3 along with Isaiah 40:11 and Hosea 11:3-4).

We can feel the tenderness, watchfulness and jealousy of motherhood here. Elsewhere in the Bible this is balanced by the strength of fatherhood:

> '... you saw how the LORD your God carried you, as a father carries his son, all the way you went...'(Deuteronomy 1:31).

Another example of God applying the character of motherhood to himself is this:

> 'Can a mother forget the baby at her breast and have no compassion on the child she has borne? Though she may forget, I will not forget you' (Isaiah 49:14-16).

Here the emphasis is on God's remembering his children. He does not forget them, indeed, the passage insists that he cannot do so. Think of a family gathering where there is much talking and laughter that blots out all external noise. Suddenly, one of the women slips out of the room; no one else has heard the cry of her baby in another part of the house, but her ear is attuned to the voice of her child. And of God the Psalmist says, 'his ears are attentive to their cry' (Psalm 34:14) and, like a human mother, God knows if our cry is a sham or if we are in real trouble!

No earthly father loves like Thee;
No mother e'er so mild,
Bears and forbears as Thou hast done
With me, Thy sinful child.
(Frederick W Faber)

Our Father's guidance

God's love is also seen in the way he guides us. A father desires the best for his children. If he is a good father he will try to guide his girl or boy into good morals because bad morals lead to unhappiness. This is a reflection of the way in which our heavenly Father shows us how to live. He said to his people in Old Testament days:

> '...I am the LORD your God who teaches you what is best for you, who directs you in the way you should go. If only you had paid attention to my commands, your peace would have been like a river, your righteousness like the waves of the sea' (Isaiah 48:17-18).

The Scriptures are God's love gift to his children, giving them guidance for their conduct in every conceivable situation they are likely to meet in this life. This is why it is very important for us to know the Bible well. When we do, we learn to think biblically and we know instinctively what we should do in very many situations. It is not normally difficult for a child to know the wishes of his or her father; problems only arise when those wishes conflict with what the child wants to do.

There are many decisions to be made, some of which are ordinary day-to-day matters, but others affect the whole course of our lives, such as our career, marriage or where we are to live. Our Father says:

> 'I will instruct you and teach you in the way you should go;
> I will counsel you and watch over you' (Psalm 32:8).

But how does he guide us? Some answers given to this question are very confusing. When we know God is dealing with us as children, guidance is not so complicated as it is often made out to be. Many Christians make very heavy weather of seeking and finding out the

Lord's will for them in given situations. Some go into a state of limbo unable to do anything until they are sure what God wants them to do. Others are distressed if they cannot discover the guiding hand of God in a specific Scripture or some unusual happening. But a child does not normally have a difficulty in knowing what his or her father wishes. Nor does a father have a problem in conveying his guidance to his child. Surely our heavenly Father can and does guide us in ways we cannot mistake.

Very young children need to be told precisely what they must do. Likewise when we are spiritual babes (1 Peter 2:2) our heavenly Father's will for us is reflected in the instruction of parents or Christian teachers. But as we grow to maturity a good earthly father will not seek to make decisions for us but rather help us to make up our own minds. This again illustrates the way our heavenly Father deals with us.

We need to beware of using the Bible in a way that bypasses our minds. For example, someone may be deciding whether to set up home in a certain village and at that moment comes upon the words 'go to the village ahead of you' (Matthew 21:2), and assumes this is the Lord's leading. Many people are tempted to take their guidance from using Scripture in that way. But this avoids the use of our minds and treats Scripture in an unnatural way. The Bible is our Father's message to us in what it teaches and the examples it gives. He shows us in the Scriptures the right principles, motives and other considerations that we must have in mind when making important decisions such as moving to another place, changing jobs or getting married. He then encourages us to work out the way ahead for ourselves.

'Do not conform any longer to the pattern of this world, but be transformed by the renewing of your mind. Then you will be able to test and approve what God's will is — his good, pleasing and perfect will' (Romans 12:2).

Questions such as 'Is this honouring to the Lord?' 'Is this helpful for my spiritual growth?' or 'Will I be able to serve the Lord better?' will be faced honestly, and, perhaps with the help of reliable friends, lead us to wise decisions.

Another parallel with human fatherhood is this. No two children are alike — not even twins! They differ in temperament, talents, understanding and many other ways. No father worthy of the name will deal with each of his children in exactly the same way; he will know the best way to handle each child. This is supremely true of our heavenly Father, and for this reason it is very unwise to lay down detailed rules for guidance. For instance, one child has lots of confidence, while another is very fearful; or, one child is quick to make decisions while another dithers so much as to try the patience of every one else who is involved. Our heavenly Father knows how best to guide each of us.

The Christian life is not one of rules and regulations, but of a relationship with a wise and loving Father. Just as a child knows how to discover the mind of a father, so God's children gradually discover how to know his will for them. This is a part of our development as the children of God. A father knows how to steer each child into the best course, so does our heavenly Father. The question is, do we want to know his way for us?

> 'If any of you lacks wisdom, he should ask God, who gives generously to all without finding fault, and it will be given to him' (James 1:6).

As children of God we can be sure our Father loves us, not only because he has assured us of his love over and over again in the Scriptures, but also because we constantly experience the evidence of that love as he cares for us and guides us in the details of our lives.

12.
Our Father's compassion

Thinking of our Father's love as we have done leads us on naturally to consider one important aspect of that love namely, his great compassion. We can read about this in both the Old and New Testaments:

> 'Because of the LORD's great love we are not consumed, for his compassion's never fail' (Lamentations 3:22).

> 'Praise be to the God and Father of our Lord Jesus Christ, the Father of compassion and the God of all comfort, who comforts us in all our troubles...' (2 Corinthians 1:3-4).

Our heavenly Father is the very source of all expressions of comfort. When we comfort one another, the very desire and ability to do so comes from him. Even when godless people are kind and compassionate, those feelings do not originate in their sinful hearts, but in God. This is one aspect of his common grace without which mankind would have destroyed itself long ago.

God is especially tender towards his children, and this is expressed in 2 Corinthians 1:3-4 we have already quoted, in the two words 'compassion' and 'comfort'.

Our Father's sympathy

The main thought of 'compassion' is sympathy. My college English and Greek tutor led the service at my induction into the pastorate at Cransford in Suffolk. Imagine the reaction of the people when his remarks began 'I am here today to express my sympathy with you'! What did he mean? Did he know something about me that would cause the people to regret calling me to lead them? No! He went on to give us an English lesson in the meaning of the word 'sympathy' which is to feel with each other both in joy and in sorrow. That is what our heavenly Father is like, he shares our joys and according to the prophet Isaiah our sorrows also:

'In all their distress he too was distressed...' (Isaiah 63:9).

There have always been, and still are Christian teachers who argue that God cannot have feelings of joy or sorrow. Their arguments are based on the unchangeable nature of God's being, character and purpose, and may seem at first sight to be convincing; but this is a case of trying to fit the truth about God into our limited human reasoning. Donald Macleod deals with the issue in this way:

'...the idea that God is a passionless, emotionally immobile being is totally unscriptural. The Bible reveals him as a God of wrath and jealousy. It also reveals him as One who has no pleasure in the death of the wicked (Ezekiel 33:11) and therefore, by implication, as One who is grieved when human beings destroy themselves. The New Testament even describes the Holy Spirit specifically as capable of grief (Ephesians 4:30). Similarly, God is revealed as One who is passionate in his love, loving the church as a husband loves his wife, extravagant in his devotion and tormented by her infidelities. These are all fundamentally important parts of the biblical portrait of God and quite irreconcilable with the view that he is emotionally inert.'
(*Behold your God:* Donald Macleod,   Christian Focus Publications)

Donald Macleod goes on to show that the idea of God having no feelings is quite inconsistent with the Bible assurance that he has pity, and indeed with the whole meaning of the crucifixion of our Lord. The fact is that God is altogether beyond our grasp and we must be willing to accept apparent contradictions about him in the Scriptures. We delight in God's unchangeableness. This is an anchor for our souls in a world of change and decay, but we must not allow ourselves to be robbed of a Father in heaven who can be grieved to the depth of his being. Through the prophet Hosea, God speaks to his people who are unfaithful to him:

'How can I give you up, O Ephraim! How can I surrender you, and cast you off, O Israel! How can I make you as Admah, or how can I treat you as Zeboiim (both destroyed with Sodom)! My heart recoils within Me, My compassion's are kindled together' (Hosea 11:8 Amplified Bible).

The picture is of one who says, 'your stupidity and waywardness made my stomach turn over'. God's heart was torn with a mixture of holy grief and loving compassion. This is the God whom Jesus came to reveal to us and of whom it is said he is able to 'sympathise with our weaknesses' (Hebrews 4:15). It is true that the Scriptures must translate truth into language we can understand, and that at times human feelings and actions are used to help us understand what God is like; but if God's compassion and sympathy are not real then our faith also is but a make-believe. We can be sure that the compassion of our heavenly Father is no mere pretence, it is real, just as surely as Jesus had compassion on the people of his day (Matthew 9:36).

At the same time our Father God can be delighted beyond words.

'The Lord your God is with you, he is mighty to save. He will take great delight in you, he will quiet you with his love, he will rejoice over you with singing' (Zephaniah 3:17).

Our Father's comfort

In 2 Corinthians 1:3-4 Paul not only says that our Father has compassion on us but also that he comforts us. Here the emphasis is on the second part of the word, and could helpfully be expressed as fortifying or strengthening. When we are in trouble we need sympathy, but that alone just leaves us where we were before; in fact, human helpers often have to say to us 'I'm sorry for you, I grieve with you, but there is nothing I can do to help you.' Thank God he is not limited in that way. His compassion is accompanied by fortifying. He gives us new inner strength to go on and to overcome our problem. When in 1966 the English soccer team played Germany in a World Cup final, the scores of the two sides were still level at the end of full time. As they waited to play extra time, they were sprawled out on the turf exhausted wondering how they could survive another period. Their manager, Alf Ramsey, strode up to them shouting, 'Get up on your feet!' They did, and went on to win. It was a good piece of psychology; it meant 'you can do it, you know you can win, show them you know you can win'. That is fortifying. Of course their resources were in themselves which they needed to discover and use, whereas our strength is in the Lord. A biblical example is God's response to Paul's repeated plea for his 'thorn in the flesh' to be removed, he said:

> 'My grace is sufficient for you, for my power is made perfect in weakness' (2 Corinthians 12:7-9).

Sympathy alone will lull us to sleep or allow us to sink into helplessness. Fortifying alone is harsh and forbidding, but sympathy and fortifying together are perfect companions. Our God is 'the Father of compassion and the God of all comfort'.

> 'We ought to turn to God for comfort, naturally and spontaneously. If my son skins his knee he runs into my arms with tears streaming down his face. He does not philosophize about whether his father cares; he comes for a cuddle. Of course, in some ways we are not children, and God's Fatherhood is not exactly like my own. (In fact, mine is but a pale imitation of his; Ephesians 3:15.) But we ought to be sufficiently childlike that we quickly turn to God for comfort when, metaphorically, we skin our knee. This is not a sign of immaturity, it is a sign of belonging.'
> (*How long, O Lord?:* D A Carson, IVP)

Don Carson goes on to say that the comfort God gives is not a mere logical attitude 'God knows best', though that is true. It is the movement of God on the soul giving a powerful sense of his love and care.

An American Christian's husband was killed in the Vietnam war. When the news of his death reached her she went to her room. After she had been there for some time her friends who were visiting were concerned enough for one of them to go and listen discreetly at her door. All that could be heard was, 'Oh Father! Oh Father! Oh my Father!' as the now widowed lady buried herself into the arms of her heavenly father. This was not a sudden desperate reaction to tragedy. Those comforting arms were well known to her from past experience of lesser troubles.

This is your God — a Father who feels for you and at the same time helps you, and whose sympathy is matched by his ability and willingness to strengthen you.

13.
Our Father talks to us

These are days in which conversation between parents and children is crowded out by homework, television and many other pursuits. Homes are places of much coming and going and there is little opportunity simply to sit and enjoy each other's company and conversation. For all too many of us this also describes our relationship with fellow Christians and above all with our heavenly Father.

A father who does not want to speak to his children is scarcely worthy of the name, and we can be sure our heavenly Father wants to speak to us. But we are so busy, not least with what we call 'the Lord's work', that sometimes he has to put us out of action for a while through illness or some other way so as to make us sit, or even lay, and listen to him. If God is our Father then we are able to enjoy conversation with him and we are foolish to deprive ourselves of that privilege. Maybe you have lost the desire to listen to your Father, and you do not enjoy his voice; in that case you need to confess it to him and ask him to restore that joy.

Sin creates a barrier

We can have no relationship at all with God as our Father until the sin barrier has been removed. This happens when we begin to trust in Jesus Christ; he gives us peace with God and the lines of communication are open:

> 'Therefore, since we have been justified through faith, we have peace with God through our Lord Jesus Christ, through whom we have gained access by faith into this grace in which we now stand...' (Romans 5:1-2).

It is good for us always to remember that our fellowship with God as our Father is continuously dependent on the mediation of Jesus Christ. When we say at the end of our prayers 'in the name of Jesus Christ' or 'for the sake of our Lord Jesus Christ' or words like that, it should be no mere formality; we should be acknowledging that Jesus Christ purchased for us our right of access to the Father.

But within this relationship there can be blockages, and if we are spiritually serious we will be sensitive to these hindrances to our communication with our Father. If children are disobedient or unruly, their relationship with their parents is unhappy and strained because their parents are grieved. So it is between us and our heavenly Father. If we are grieving him by some sin in which we are persisting, then his voice will not be so clear to us and we will not welcome what he is saying. Our Father is grieved and we are out of tune with him. We must not let such a situation go on. We must repent, turn from our disobedience, no matter what form it takes and at whatever cost. This will clear the air and our joyful fellowship with our Father will be renewed. The apostle John wrote:

'If we claim to have fellowship with him yet walk in darkness, we lie and do not live by the truth. But if we walk in the light, as he is in the light, we have fellowship with one another, and the blood of Jesus, his Son, purifies us from all sin. If we claim to be without sin, we deceive ourselves and the truth is not in us. If we confess our sins, he is faithful and just and will forgive us our sins and purify us from all unrighteousness' (1 John 1:6-9).

We often apply these words to unconverted people and it is right for us to do so, but we should not forget that originally they were addressed to people who were already children of God. Lack of peace and joy in many Christians' lives arises from their failure to distinguish between God as their judge and God as their Father. God is our judge and we must stand before him one day. We will be dumb in the face of every exposure of our sinfulness, but at one and the same time we will be at peace because our mediator, the Lord Jesus Christ, will show that he suffered our punishment in our place.

'Who is he that condemns? Christ Jesus who died — more than that, who was raised to life — is at the right hand of God and is also interceding for us' (Romans 8:34).

Because of what Jesus has done for us we can never be banished by
God as our judge; we are no longer condemned sinners but children
in a happy relationship with God as our Father. As soon as trouble
begins to arise, some of God's children immediately and foolishly
begin to think that God is punishing them as their judge; and when
they sin, they are instantly afraid that they will again come under his
condemnation. If only they could realise that this is impossible since
Christ has died for them, they would not live in such fear.

> '... there is now no condemnation for those who are in Christ
> Jesus' (Romans 8:1).

As a faithful, loving Father, the Lord chastises his children. We see
this in the carrying away of the Israelite nation into the captivity of
Babylon. The prophet Jeremiah explained that the reason for this
was their unfaithfulness in worshipping other gods and relying for
strength and protection on other nations:

> '... How gladly would I treat you like sons and give you a
> desirable land, the most beautiful inheritance of any nation.
> I thought you would call me 'Father' and not turn away from
> following me. But like a woman unfaithful to her husband
> so you have been unfaithful to me, O house of Israel,
> declares the LORD' (Jeremiah 3:19-20).

Our Father's love does not falter, as we can see in the remarkable
promise he made to his people even before they were taken into the
Babylonian captivity:

> 'Yet the Israelites will be like the sand on the seashore,
> which cannot be measured or counted. In the place where it
> was said to them "You are not my people," they will be
> called "sons of the living God"' (Hosea 1:10).

All this anticipates the picture that Jesus gives of the Father who
welcomed home his erring son (Luke 15:11-32). A painful experience may be a punishment for an unbeliever, but in a child of God
it can never be punishment. It is true we speak of a father punishing
his child for wrong-doing, but we do well in understanding Christian
experience to apply to the notion of punishment only to unbelievers.

A child of God will suffer loving and purposeful correction and it is best to call this chastisement because our Lord Jesus Christ has suffered the punishment of our sins for us. We are God's children — we will grieve him and he will chastise us (see chapter 16) — but he will never abandon or disown us.

Our Father's voice

There are not many direct references in Scripture to God speaking to his people as their Father. Nevertheless, rightly understood, the whole of the Bible is the voice of God to be heard by his children; it is the 'word of encouragement that addresses you as sons' (Hebrews 12:5). How then does our Father speak to us through the Scriptures?

Many people who read the Bible as a piece of literature because of its beautiful language, or as a means of comfort and consolation, never hear God speaking to them through its teaching. So how do we hear the voice of God through the Scriptures? The answer is that although the whole Bible is the Word of God (2 Timothy 3:15-17), whether we heed it or not, he is able to apply the words we happen to be reading at any time to our minds, hearts and consciences in such a way that we know what in particular he is saying to us. Jesus Christ prayed:

'... I praise you, Father, Lord of heaven and earth, because you have hidden these things from the wise and learned, and revealed them to little children. Yes, Father, for this was your good pleasure' (Matthew 11:25-26).

Also, when Peter declared Jesus to be the Son of the Living God, Jesus replied:

'Blessed are you, Simon son of Jonah, for this was not revealed to you by man, but by my Father in heaven' (Matthew 16:16-17).

Thus we see that our heavenly Father opens our minds to receive his truth. We need to read the Bible with humble dependence on the Holy Spirit to give us understanding and enabling us to apply what we are reading to ourselves.

Near the beginning of our Christian life we can hear our Father saying to us 'Your sins are forgiven, you are my child'. Often he uses a Scripture to convince us that this is what he is saying to us. Although many Scriptures were quoted at the time I was converted and baptised, it was not until two years later that a text came to me unexpectedly and fixed itself indelibly on my mind and heart; 'Being confident of this, that he who began a good work in you will carry it on to completion until the day of Christ Jesus' (Philippians 1:6). I still find it difficult to read or quote that text without a feeling of excitement, and preaching on it is sheer delight! Thank you, Father!

We certainly will not hear God speaking to us through the Scriptures unless we read them with submission and obedience. God says:

> 'This is the one I esteem: he who is humble and contrite in spirit, and trembles at my word' (Isaiah 66:2; see also Psalm 25:14; Proverbs 3:32).

In the same vein Jesus said:

> 'If anyone chooses to do God's will, he will find out whether my teaching comes from God or whether I speak on my own' (John 7:17).

We see then the importance of both submission and obedience to God as essential to our understanding the Scriptures and hearing him speaking to us.

There is the ever present danger of using texts out of harmony with their plain meaning; the result of this is certainly not to receive a message from God. To avoid this danger we must always try to understand the meaning of a text or passage in its own setting; we can then go on to ask the Lord to help us to see how the teaching applies to us in our situation. We need to learn to think biblically. The Gospels show us how the mind of Jesus was saturated with Scripture, and it is when our minds are full of Bible teaching that we know more readily what our Father is saying to us.

We must also remember that our Father has given us the Holy Spirit to help us to understand the Scriptures, and especially to see Jesus Christ revealed in every part of the Bible. Jesus said to his disciples:

'I have much more to say to you, more than you can now bear. But when he, the Spirit of truth, comes, he will guide you into all truth. He will not speak on his own; he will speak only what he hears, and he will tell you what is yet to come. He will bring glory to me by taking from what is mine and making it known to you. All that belongs to the Father is mine. That is why I said the Spirit will take from what is mine and make it known to you' (John 16:12-15).

Direct revelations

So far I have assumed that our Father normally speaks to us through the Scriptures. The question arises as to whether we may also hear his voice directly through some impression on our minds, a vision or some other form of direct revelation. First of all, we must never separate the Holy Spirit from the Scriptures in such a way as to put supposed revelations from him above the teaching of the Bible. Since the Holy Spirit is the author of Scripture (2 Timothy 3:16; 2 Peter 1:20-21) it is not possible for him to contradict himself by giving us ideas that are contrary to Scripture. Nevertheless, it is clear that, both in Scripture and in the experience of Christians throughout history, God has sometimes spoken to his people in dreams (Genesis 37:5,9) and visions (Daniel 8:1-2).

The problem here is that human nature craves for the unusual and the sensational, and too often believers have fastened on to the possibility of God using such means and have not been satisfied until they could claim this kind of experience for themselves. Quite apart from what happened at his conversion (Acts 9:1-12) Paul had a vision at Troas (Acts 16:9) and other extraordinary experiences (2 Corinthians 12:1-6), but notice that this was not frequently repeated. He did not ask for such things to happen, nor did he wait for them as though they were essential to him. He was reticent to speak of them and he certainly did not even hint that others should have the same experiences.

Interest in dreams and visions tends to increase at times when the truth is not being preached with the authority of the Holy Spirit. In the Old Testament Jeremiah came upon people who preferred their dreams to his teaching.

'I have heard what the prophets say who prophesy lies in my name. They say "I had a dream! I had a dream!" How long will this continue in the hearts of these lying prophets, who prophesy the delusions of their own minds? They think the dreams they tell one another will make my people forget my name, just as their fathers forgot my name through Baal worship. Let the prophet who has a dream tell his dream, but let the one who has my word speak it faithfully. "For what has straw to do with grain?" declares the LORD. "Is not my word like fire," declares the LORD, "and like a hammer that breaks a rock in pieces?' (Jeremiah 23:25-29).

This passage encourages us to ask five questions about a dream or vision:

1. Does it merely confirm the well known ideas of the dreamer (26)?
2. Does it lead to the knowledge of God (27)?
3. Does it harmonise with the known truth of God (27, 28)?
4. Is is spiritually nourishing like grain rather than straw (28)?
5. Does it cleanse our lives like a purifying fire (29)?

Our Father normally speaks to us through the Scriptures, and the Scriptures nowhere teach us to seek special revelations; rather they warn us to test them very carefully (1 John 4:1). In fact one positive test will be that the experience comes to us unsought and unexpectedly.

Quite apart from dreams, visions and similar experiences, our Father can and often does prompt our minds; he can steer our thinking in the way he wants us to go. While I have been writing this book and asking him to help me and guide me, whole sections of it have opened up while I have been on my morning walk, or at other times. This kind of thing is so undramatic that we do not realise it is the Lord's answer to our prayers, by guiding our thoughts into unexpected channels. Again, these promptings must be tested by Scripture — 'test everything' (1 Thessalonians 5:21).

While I was involved in Christian radio my colleagues and I were challenged to produce material rooted in the basic concepts of the Christian faith. The result was several years of weekly programmes under the title 'God Speaks'. This is gloriously basic; my Father talks to me, and he speaks in language I can understand.

14.
Our Father listens to us

Happy and secure family life is built up on relationships and the essence of relationship is the sharing of common interests in uninhibited conversation. This is what a church is meant to be like, and prayer meetings should be gatherings of the family around our heavenly Father. There is no reason why we should not pray to Jesus Christ and to the Holy Spirit, but the normal pattern is:

'Through him (Jesus Christ) we both (Jews and Gentiles) have access to the Father by one Spirit' (Ephesians 2:18).

The idea of the family gathering is not to be lost even in our personal prayer life because Jesus taught us to pray 'Our Father...', so even when we speak to the Father as individuals we are not to forget that we do so as part of the Christian family.

The setting for conversation between us and the Father is our heart. Jesus said:

'If anyone loves me, he will obey my teaching. My Father will love him, and we will come to him and make our home with him' (John 14:23).

The place where we pray and the time we choose may have some effect on our prayers, but since our Father has made his home in our heart the time and place where we pray are not important. It is undoubtedly good to have regular prayer times when our Father speaks to us and we to him, but there is no time or situation when he is not accessible or refuses to hear us.

Nothing should be excluded from our conversations with our heavenly Father. Our prayer life needs to be liberated from formality and from the narrow range of topics to which we are too often confined. Except perhaps when we are asking for some special favour, we do not normally rehearse what we are going to say as children to a human father. The words tumble out, as we range from one thing to another, and we re-act to what our father says to us. If only we could think of prayer like that, and in practice enjoy that kind of prayer life more and more!

A model prayer

Our Lord has given us a model for prayer to the Father:

> 'Our Father in heaven,
> hallowed be your name
> your kingdom come,
> your will be done
>   on earth, as it is in heaven.
> Give us to-day our daily bread.
> Forgive us our debts,
>   as we also have forgiven our debtors.
> And lead us not into temptation
> but deliver us from the evil one'
> (Matthew 6:9-13; see also Luke 11:2-4).

We see immediately the scope he gives us. There is no reason why we should not use this prayer as it stands, but that is not the limit of our Lord's purpose. He has given us here a kind of outline to fill in, and as we do so we shall find our minds ranging far and wide. There will be praise, intercession for gospel work throughout the world, request for material and daily needs, desire to be in harmony with God and with all people, concern for testing situations and longing for holiness.

'Our Father in heaven'

This opening clause of the outline prayer, instantly establishes the atmosphere of prayer, the attitude with which we should come into the presence of our heavenly Father. We see here in the greatest possible simplicity a blend that nevertheless seems so impossible for many of God's children to understand or achieve. It is a blend of reverence and liberty, of awe and love, of submission and joy (Proverbs 23:26). God is our Father and he is in heaven. God is in heaven and he is our Father. Our Father is on the throne and we are members of the royal family. Jesus leaves us in no doubt that we must not worship anyone else:

> 'Do not call anyone on earth "father" for you have one Father, and he is in heaven' (Matthew 23:9).

If, when we pray, we remember that our Father is in heaven, this will not only give us a sense of awe and reverence, it will also excite the admiration and praise which are a very important parts of prayer. Remember too, that Jesus addressed God as 'Holy Father' (John 17:11); this will take away pride, arrogance and self-assertiveness in prayer. We will reflect on our sinfulness and therefore our unworthiness to come into a holy Father's presence, and our complete dependence on the mediation of Jesus Christ.

The exalted position of our Father will also give us confidence that he is able to give us what we ask for. Jesus has given us tremendous promises about this:

> 'You did not choose me, but I chose you and appointed you to go and bear fruit — fruit that will last. Then the Father will give you whatever you ask in my name' (John 15:16).

> 'I tell you the truth, my Father will give you whatever you ask in my name' (John 16:23).

> 'I tell you that if two of you on earth agree about anything you ask for, it will be done for you by my Father in heaven' (Matthew 18:19).

When Jesus says 'in my name' he indicates that our requests must be in harmony with his mind and character and in harmony also with our union with him. This should not inhibit our petitions, but nevertheless lead us to examine our motives and to yield willingly to what our Father deems best for us.

'Abba, Father'

This leads us to consider the effect of remembering that it is to a father that we are praying. Jesus addressed his Father as 'Abba' (Mark 14:36) but what does this mean? There is no doubt it was the word used in everyday life in Jewish homes. From this fact some people have drawn the conclusion that it gives us liberty to address God as 'Daddy' in the same sense that we use the term in our society today. But this is to ignore the fact that a Jewish father held a position of much greater authority than our fathers do today. Children were dependent on their father, and under his authority; he was in every way the head of the household so long as he lived. The result was an attitude by the children of genuine and deep affection and also of respect and submission. This attitude is reflected in our Lord's prayer to the Father in Gethsemane:

> 'Abba, Father, ... everything is possible for you. Take this cup from me. Yet not what I will, but what you will'
> (Mark 14:36).

This is the attitude we must seek, the freedom of children with their father along with the respect and submission that come from both admiration and a sense of dependence.

Paul tells us that the warrant and ability to cry 'Abba Father' is the work of the Holy Spirit in us:

> '... you did not receive a spirit that makes you a slave again to fear, but you received the Spirit of sonship. And by him we cry, "Abba, Father"' (Romans 8:15).

> 'Because you are sons, God sent the Spirit of his Son into our hearts, the Spirit who calls out, "Abba, Father"'
> (Galatians 4:6).

Some people understand the apostle to mean that this is a special work of the Holy Spirit in the experience of believers after their conversion. Others of us believe the Spirit, having begun his work in us when he entered our lives and gave us spiritual life, gradually leads us to deeper understanding and experience of fellowship with God as our heavenly Father.

Either way there can be no doubt that all of us need to seek a more intimate fellowship with God as our Father. We should not be content with a superficial acquaintance, or with a perfunctory prayer life. To grow in this relationship is to grow in grace, and to enter more fully into the experience of eternal life which is nothing less than a never-ending exploration into the heart of God (John 17:3).

All this will naturally lead to greater confidence in prayer. We will discover that God is a better Father to us than any human father can be to his children. As Jesus said,

> 'If you, then, though you are evil, know how to give good gifts to your children, how much more will your Father in heaven give good gifts to those who ask him!' (Matthew 7:11).

'hallowed be your name'

Jesus now directs us to glorify of the Father. God is the only person in the whole universe that has the right to seek his own glory. He made the world for that very purpose and the whole plan of salvation is designed likewise to be to the praise of his glory (Romans 11:33-36; Ephesians 1:4-6). If glory is given to anything or anyone else this detracts from what is due to God alone. Unconverted people resent this idea, and for the most part reject it altogether. They may attend church and recite this prayer as a kind of religious ritual, but their hearts are not in it. Not only so, some believers seem to think that loading them with blessings is what God is 'for.' O for a heart that has only one ambition — that God is glorified!

The 'name' of God stands for the glory of his person and character. As we see from other Scriptures:

> 'O LORD, our Lord, how majestic is your name in all the earth! You have set your glory above the heavens' (Psalm 8:1).

> 'Ascribe to the LORD the glory due to his name; worship the LORD in the splendour of his holiness' (Psalm 29:2).

To 'hallow' something is to set it apart as very special. So, at the beginning of this prayer, our Lord is teaching us to praise God. This praise should express our conviction that our Father is apart from and above all others in his excellency, holiness, love and mercy. Furthermore, to pray this prayer means that we want everyone else to do the same. True Christians will use this prayer as an opportunity to examine every part of their lives, private, home, church, business and leisure, and to ask for the Father's enabling to glorify him in all these areas. If we are sincere about this we will soon examine our motives in life, and ask ourselves why we do what we do. Is it our increasing desire to bring him praise in everything without exception? Our failure to do this often means that our Father's name is not hallowed but rather despised by the people around us:

> 'God's name is blasphemed among the Gentiles because of you' (Romans 2:24).

It was this that Daniel was concerned about. He confessed the sins of God's people and pleaded with the Lord for his pardon and restoration on the basis that the honour of God's name was at stake:

> 'Now our God, hear the prayers and petitions of your servant. For your sake, O Lord, look with favour on your desolate sanctuary. Give ear, O God, and hear; open your eyes and see the desolation of the city that bears your Name. We do not make our requests to you because we are righteous, but because of your great mercy. O Lord, listen! O Lord, forgive! O Lord, hear and act! For your sake, O my God, do not delay, because your city and your people bear your Name' (Daniel 9:17-19).

Our desire for our Father's glory should be an end in itself, not a means to get something from him. And yet, in the nature of things if God is glorified man always receives the benefit. 'The fear of the LORD is the beginning of wisdom' (Psalm 111:10); as soon as people put God first in their affections and endeavours their lives will be blessed beyond measure.

15.
Our Father's interests

For many years friends of mine tried to interest me in the inner workings of tape recorders and mixing desks. My reply was always, "I do not understand and I do not want to understand, I have no interest in such things!" We have been thinking of prayer as conversation between our heavenly Father and his children; such conversation is a sharing of things in which we have a mutual interest. A person who is unregenerate has little or no interest in the same things as God; such matters are a foreign world to an unbeliever. A true Christian wants to love what God loves and to hate what God hates. Seen like this, true prayer can only take place between God and someone who is born again.

A nurse arrives home to share with his or her partner the successes and failures of the day on the ward; perhaps before marriage the partner had no interest in (even a strong aversion to!) such things, but their love relationship is important and gradually there is a bending of the mind to listen, understand, sympathise and even enthuse over the daily bulletin. In the same way a Christian loves the Father, and wants to be in harmony with his desires and concerns. This is where the outline prayer Jesus gave us is so helpful; after expressions of praise and worship it introduces us to those matters that our Father wants us to talk to him about. First of all, his kingdom:

'your kingdom come'

God will be glorified when his kingdom comes, so our common interest with our Father is the spread of his kingdom throughout the world. His kingdom comes when he begins his reign in the hearts of men and women and this happens when they hear the gospel and receive Jesus Christ. Once more we see the tremendous scope of this prayer, it ranges world-wide and embraces every rightful means used to spread the gospel. We should not forget that, quite apart from this model prayer, our Lord has given us specific instructions to pray for workers to be directed into missionary enterprise throughout the world which includes, of necessity, every part of our own country.

> 'When he saw the crowds, he had compassion on them because they were harassed and helpless, like sheep without a shepherd. Then he said to his disciples, "The harvest is plentiful but the workers are few. Ask the Lord of the harvest, therefore, to send out workers into his harvest field"' (Matthew 9:36-38).

This is also in harmony with the apostle Paul's repeated request for prayer for himself and his fellow workers in the gospel:

> '...pray for us, too, that God may open a door for our message, so that we may proclaim the mystery of Christ, for which I am in chains. Pray that I may proclaim it clearly, as I should' (Colossians 4:3-4; see also Ephesians 6:19; 2 Thessalonians 3:1).

How does it come about that so often we wonder what to pray for and prayer meetings are frequently so flat and silent?

'your will be done on earth as it is in heaven'

These first petitions teach us what should take the prime place in our prayer life; the things of greatest interest to our Father should also be first in our thoughts. When the gospel has its effect in peoples' lives they begin to want to do his will, and a community of such people is a piece of heaven on earth. This is the best evidence of the work of the Holy Spirit in the human heart; we no longer want our own way, rather we want to do God's will. The essence of sin is disobedience, and the essence of holiness is obedience. So we have an interest in every life that touches ours in any way. We want the grace of obedience ourselves, and we want to see that grace at work in every one else. The scope is without limit.

This petition is also an expression of love for the people around us, though they may not want to acknowledge it. The collapse of morality in society has accelerated as the influence of the Bible has diminished. This in turn has resulted in all kinds of pain and distress. Consequently, one of the most loving things we can do is to pray that people will increasingly submit to the will of God; such prayer should also be accompanied by earnest efforts to spread the gospel.

'give us today our daily bread'

The abrupt switch from spiritual and eternal concerns to 'daily bread' is in itself instructive. While God's glory should indeed be our priority, this is a long way from saying that our Father has little interest in our material needs. In this model prayer the two areas are mentioned almost in the same breath. There is nothing outside the scope of our Father's concern for us, and therefore there should be no limit to the things we share with him.

This part of the prayer, as much as the rest, is a clear indication of the difference between those who are God's children and those who are not. In contrast to others true Christians relate the whole of life to God, we do not separate 'religion' from the rest of our experience. Our prayers should have a healthy balance and we can be sure that our Father does not lose interest no matter what we share with him.

Furthermore, whereas people who are not God's children take the gifts of life for granted, we acknowledge that everything we have comes from God and that we are dependent on him for all the necessities of life. Also, we know that we do not deserve any of these things and therefore we do not demand anything from God. We accept his right to give or to withhold whatever our request might be.

This prayer also involves us in the needs of others. We are to pray 'give us... our' — so our petitions must range over all the physical and material needs of our friends, and further still to the deprived and famine-stricken people of the world. All these things we should share with our heavenly Father.

'forgive us our debts'

The remainder of the prayer is largely about personal spiritual needs. As we have seen, there is no possibility that our sins as believers will bring us again under condemnation and eternal punishment, but this must not make us insensitive to the way our daily failures and shortcomings affect our relationship with our Father. So as we come into his presence we remember that he is a holy Father and that he wants us to be holy, indeed, he has saved us through Jesus Christ so that we can be holy. Our love for him, similarly, will determine that we abhor everything in our lives which grieves and offends him. Such things are 'debts' because they are moral obligations which we cannot meet, and because they make us indebted to God for his pardon. At this point prayer becomes an exercise in self-examination as we acknowledge our sins and ask for our Father's forgiveness.

> 'Search me, O God, and know my heart; test me and know my anxious thoughts. See if there is any offensive way in me, and lead me in the way everlasting' (Psalm 139:23-24).

The further we go on in Christian experience the more space we may well give to this; we will see ourselves more and more as God sees us, and the greater will be our sense of the seriousness and depth of our need for forgiveness.

'as we also have forgiven our debtors'

At first sight these words may startle us because they seem to contradict the great teaching of justification by faith only, and to take us back to salvation by works. This impression seems to be confirmed by the teaching of Jesus following the prayer:

> 'For if you forgive men when they sin against you, your heavenly Father will also forgive you. But if you do not forgive men their sins, your Father will not forgive your sins' (Matthew 6:14-15).

Our Lord himself puts much emphasis on faith as the means of receiving eternal life (John 3:16; 6:47), and the epistles are adamant that:

> 'it is by grace you have been saved through faith — and this not from yourselves, it is the gift of God — not by works, so that no one can boast' (Ephesians 2:8-9; Galatians 2:15-16).

What then does Jesus mean in this part of the prayer? It is all part of the self-examination mentioned a few moments ago. First of all, if we are children of God we will reflect something of his character in the way we live, and nothing is clearer in our Father's character than his readiness to forgive. We will not live this out to perfection, but the character will be recognisable in us. If not, it has to be questioned whether we are Christians at all, and that therefore we have no right to come to God as children to a father. But alas! true Christians are often unforgiving and our Father will not let us get away with this. He will withhold his smile until we have put things right. This is a serious matter and too many of us are careless about it, which is surprising when we think of all the exhortations in Scripture about forgiving one another.

> 'Be kind and compassionate to one another, forgiving each other, just as in Christ God forgave you. Be imitators of God, therefore, as dearly beloved children' (Ephesians 4:32-51; see also Matthew 18:21-35).

'lead us not into temptation'

This cannot mean that God may put us into certain situations with the intention that we will fall into sin, and that therefore we must ask him not to do so (James 1:13). Furthermore, it is unlikely that we are to ask God not to cause us to succumb to testing situations by doubting or departing from him. More likely this prayer is for strengthening so that we do not allow testing situations to lead us into sin.

The Scriptures leave us in no doubt that we must be tested and tried by persecution, opposition and all kinds of trials from the world, the flesh and the devil:

'Dear friends, do not be surprised at the painful trial you are suffering, as though something strange were happening to you' (1 Peter 4:12; see also John 16:33).

Our Father has purpose in such trials, for example purifying, strengthening our faith, and weaning us away from love of the world.

'...for a little while you may have had to suffer grief in all kinds of trials. These have come so that your faith — of greater worth than gold, which perishes even though refined by fire — may be proved genuine and may result in praise, glory and honour when Jesus Christ is revealed' (1 Peter 1:6-7).

We know our weaknesses sufficiently (or we should do!) to distrust our own ability to endure and to benefit from severe testing; so we are to pray for the Lord's strength. In fact one great purpose of these trials is for us to prove our Father's power and faithfulness and so to increase our love and devotion to him.

'deliver us from the evil one'

In every testing situation our arch enemy, the devil, is lurking in the shadows (Matthew 4:1; 2 Corinthians 2:10-11). He will do his utmost to cause us to stumble and to destroy our Christian life. Left to ourselves we are no match for him; we need our Father's protection and strengthening. Sometimes we fall and it would appear that the devil has won a great victory, but our Father is able to rescue us.

Notice that in a sense, this is a prayer before the event occurs. When we are overwhelmed with trouble it is difficult to think clearly, so it is as well to pray this prayer constantly before a sudden onset of fiery trial; this can come from our own sinful nature, from the world around us or directly from Satan himself. So, in effect, this is a prayer for holiness and as such gives us once again limitless scope of matters to share with our heavenly Father. He is certainly interested in our sanctification and he is delighted when we talk to him about that.

'...we instructed you how to live in order to please God... It
is God's will that you should be sanctified...'
(1Thessalonians 4:1-3).

Notice again the use of the plural 'us'. This is a reminder that all the
things we pray for ourselves under this heading we should also pray
for our brothers and sisters in Christ. This is what made the apostle
Paul's prayers so great (e.g. Ephesians 3:14-21; Colossians 1:9-14).

'yours is the kingdom, and the power and the glory for ever, Amen'

(NIV margin).

We cannot be certain if these words formed a conclusion to this
model prayer, but they are very appropriate. We can do no better
than use them to remind us of our Father's greatness. This is not a
petition but statement of fact uttered to the Father's praise. This
superb ending is strengthening to our faith. When we say 'Amen!'
this should not be a mere formality; it is intended to underline our
prayers with the conviction that our Father will do what we have
asked him. To pray like this is to confirm that our Father is gloriously
able to do 'immeasurably more than all we ask or imagine'
(Ephesians 3:20), and that he can and will advance all his purposes
in our lives and in the whole universe.

Also thoughts and words like these enable us to leave our time
of prayer with praise, joy and hope in our hearts. We should always
go on our way rejoicing. Our Father is really great, the greatest of all,
he should be a sheer delight to us.

A happy relationship with our Father God depends to a large extent
on our minds and hearts being in harmony with his interests. When
we share the interest of his honour, his kingdom and his gospel, then
prayer becomes a joy and fellowship with God our Father a reality.

16.
Our Father's Discipline

The Bible teaches us that fathers should discipline their children:

> 'He who spares the rod hates his son, but he who loves him is careful to discipline him.' (Proverbs 13:24; see also 19:18; 22:15; 23:13-14).

Such an idea is a shock to many people nowadays, it may be even most offensive to them. This is understandable if discipline is understood and exercised solely in terms of punishment for wrong doing. But there is more to discipline than punishment for disobedience; the 'rod' is by no means the whole of discipline; at the same time this is not to be entirely excluded from parental responsibility.

Our modern world has fallen into two kinds of extreme in these matters, as in so many other things. One extreme is either to see the need for punishment with no thought for the correction and improvement of the offender, or the whole notion of punishment is excluded in favour of aiming at reformation. In society, and families, both punishment and reformation are needed and this reflects our heavenly Father's dealings with us. The other extreme is either brutality on the one hand or indulgence on the other; there is much brutality and child abuse arising from lust and self-centredness, impatience and hardened consciences. But there is much indulgence, in which there is no correction and a child is allowed to run free and, in most cases as a result, to run wild. In the end this is as unkind as brutality and often leads to as much pain and misery even if of a different kind. Children who are gently but firmly guided and corrected are generally happier than those who are never chastened; also they are less likely to become unruly and a nuisance to society.

Because of these problems many people have difficulty in understanding God as a Father, seeing him either as a tyrant or rather like an indulgent grandparent. For this reason also, Christians are not generally sensitive to the hand of God in their lives. We re-act to the things that happen to us, pleasant or unpleasant, in a way that is no different from people who are not Christians. We take good things for granted and fail to thank God for his kindness to us, his undeserving children. Or when life is hard we complain that we do not deserve such painful experiences with bitter words, 'What have I done to deserve this?' or we shrug our shoulders with 'I suppose these things are sent to try us'. We do not seriously examine ourselves to discover why our loving heavenly Father has led us through such a rough patch. We need to recover this sense of the direct intervention of God our Father in our lives and to be grateful that he does so.

Purpose of discipline

From the moment we receive new life from the Father, he begins the process of transforming us. From now on every experience has purpose and meaning; this thought in itself makes the Christian life different from life without the knowledge of God. This is why so many people seem to wander around in a daze wondering what meaning there can possibly be to life. There is no meaning apart from God and there is no lasting satisfaction apart from life lived with God as our heavenly Father. Viewed like this the Christian life is very attractive indeed. The ultimate purpose of all that happens to us as Christians is set out perfectly for us in Romans 8:28-30:

> '...we know that in all things God works for the good of those who love him, who have been called according to his purpose. For those God foreknew he also predestined to be conformed to the likeness of his Son, that he might be the firstborn among many brothers. And those he predestined he also called; those he justified, he also glorified'.

We are to become like Jesus Christ; this at the same time prepares us for eternal glory, and all that happens to us has this aim. As Paul says in another place, 'Our light and momentary troubles are achieving for us an eternal glory that outweighs them all' (2 Corinthians 4:17).

Along the way there is another purpose and that is to make us useful in the work and witness to which the Lord calls us. This can be seen in Jesus' dealings with his disciples and in the experience of a man like Paul; as we read their stories we can see how the things that happened to them prepared them for their gospel work. Our Lord gives us teaching about this in his picture of the vine, its branches and its fruit:

> 'I am the true vine, and my Father is the gardener... Every branch that does bear fruit he prunes so that it will be even more fruitful' (John 15:1-2).

So we see that the painful experiences of life are our Father's pruning knife, and his design is that in the end we will be better Christians and more useful to him than we were before.

Need for correction

We also need correction. Children are not naturally good. Left to themselves they do all kinds of wrong things. Christians have a new nature, but they also have the residue of the old nature and there is a conflict between the two (Galatians 5:16-17); this is one of the ways we can know that we are born again, because without the new birth there is no conflict with the old nature. There is in all God's children the potential for pride, self-will, disobedience and unfaithfulness, as the Lord said of the people in Jeremiah's day:

> '... how gladly would I treat you like sons and give you a desirable land, the most beautiful inheritance of any nation. I thought you would call me Father and not turn away from following me. But like a woman unfaithful to her husband, so you have been unfaithful to me' (Jeremiah 3:19-20).

All too often we grieve and offend our heavenly Father. He is too loving to allow such things to go uncorrected.

> 'My son, do not make light of the Lord's discipline, and do not lose heart when he rebukes you, because the Lord disciplines those he loves, and he punishes everyone he

accepts as a son. Endure hardship as discipline; God is treating you as sons. For what son is not disciplined by his father? If you are not disciplined (and everyone undergoes discipline), then you are illegitimate children and not true sons. Moreover, we have all had human fathers who disciplined us and we respected them for it. How much more should we submit to the Father of our spirits and live! Our fathers disciplined us for a little while as they thought best but God disciplines us for our good, that we may share in his holiness. No discipline seems pleasant at the time, but painful. Later on, however, it produces a harvest of righteousness and peace for those who have been trained by it' (Hebrews 12:5-11).

These verses teach us that if we are being corrected we can draw the conclusion that the Lord is dealing with us as his children. This is very assuring. We are also encouraged by at least two contrasts between human fatherhood and our relationship with God as our Father. One is that our human fathers are sometimes unfair or unwise in their treatment of us, but our heavenly Father is always just and he is never mistaken. The other contrast is in the outcome. The benefits of the endeavours of human fathers are good but relate only to life on earth, whereas our Father God's treatment of us results in eternal blessings.

Correction by its very nature is painful. We do not like to be told we are wrong, that our conduct is not acceptable, or that we are letting our Father and his family down. If these corrections do not hurt us there must be a question as to whether our Christian profession is genuine. When there is an element of chastening in our Father's dealings with us it hurts; it is meant to, or else it will not achieve its purpose.

The means our Father uses

By one means or another our Father will train us for his work, correct us, chastise us, purge us of corruption and make us holy. Sometimes more than one of these aims is intended in the same painful experience. But what kind of experience might this be? The list is endless because our Father always suits his methods to our individual needs and personalities. In the case of the people to whom the letter to the Hebrews was written, it seems to have been persecution. For Peter it was the shame of his unseemly and cowardly conduct being exposed (Matthew 26:69-75). Failure of high expectations, sudden tragedy or loss, serious illness, disruption of relationships — these are some of the means God uses.

But we must be willing to learn from these experiences and submit to our Father's correction. This submission is not a fatalistic acceptance of something we could not avoid, rather it involves examining ourselves with a view to understanding what God is saying to us, and then doing whatever is necessary in response. We may not always know immediately the purpose our Father intends (notice the 'later on' in Hebrews 12:11); in that case one of the immediate lessons to learn will be patience.

It is important to remember that painful experiences are not always, perhaps not often, chastisement for specific sins. This will be revealed by honest self-examination and if no obvious disobedience or unfaithfulness comes to light, we may assume that our Father has other corrective or training purposes in mind. But, if we know ourselves as we should, we will not have to 'invent' sins to explain the Lord's dealings with us. We will be aware of sin clinging around us constantly and seek the Lord's forgiveness and cleansing (1 John 1:8-9).

Our Father is patient

Of one thing we may be absolutely certain, our Father's dealings with us as his children are always loving and patient, and always perfectly match our need. He does not cause us any pain unnecessarily, nor does he cause us more pain than is necessary. It may be that we are not listening to what he is saying to us and are persisting in our waywardness; then, in love, our Father may have to 'turn up the heat'. He sometimes has to 'speak with a voice that wakes the dead' to make us listen.

Sometimes we see a radical change for the better in the life of a fellow believer. He or she is more humble, more committed to godliness and Christian service. Or perhaps a preacher suddenly begins to be more sympathetic and more effective in his sermons. When things like that happen we will often find the explanation in some painful experience through which the person has passed. It may have been some physical problem or difficulty in the family, or in other circumstances, and the result has been a refining and mellowing which is what God intended. But this would never have happened apart from the trial which had to be suffered first.

If we are God's children he is determined to prepare us for glory and to bring us there at last and an essential part of that preparation is his loving discipline. He will have his way with us; he has begun the work, he will finish it, and when he has we will thank him and praise him throughout eternity. In anticipation we should begin to do that now.

17.
Our Father's example

We have been drawing some lessons about God as our heavenly Father from our experience of human fathers. This has not been wrong; it is always helpful to begin with what we know to enlighten us about something we know less about; this is what parables do. But the danger here is to transfer the weaknesses and failings, not to say the sins, of human fathers to our understanding of what God is like. So we must now see how the perfect Fatherhood of God is, or should be, the pattern for the human variety. Some people think this is the meaning of Paul's words:

> '... I kneel before the Father, from whom all fatherhood in heaven and on earth derives its name' (Ephesians 3:14-15 NIV margin).

It may be that the apostle is saying that all human fatherhood has its origin in God himself and that therefore he is the example for all human fathers to follow. Whether or not this is how we should understand the text, the fact remains that the world would be a better place if fathers were more Godlike in their fatherhood. This is an effect of the gospel we rarely mention. All kinds of political and social solutions are being attempted to cure the many ills in family life, and this is commendable, but the best remedy of all is the gospel through which fathers come to know God as their heavenly Father, and immediately have him as their pattern. As Tom Smail says:

> 'To know God as Father makes us different kinds of fathers, conditioned not just by our culture but by our experience of God' (*The forgotten Father*: Tom Smail, Hodder & Stoughton).

This is the very outcome of the gospel that is singled out by the prophet Malachi. The coming of the gospel began with John the Baptist, and Malachi says:

> 'He will turn the hearts of the fathers to their children, and
> the hearts of the children to their fathers' (Malachi 4:6; see
> also Luke 1:17).

At the very least these words must mean that there would be a transformation in the relationship between fathers and children, and children with their fathers.

Fathers, love your children

The first and most obvious characteristic of God's fatherhood is his love for his children. Jesus said that he did not have to persuade the Father to love us because,

> '... the Father himself loves you...' (John 16:27; see also
> 1 John 4:8-10).

In a world of pressures on time and energy it is all too easy for fathers not to spend time with their children. The perfect pattern is of our heavenly Father who is never too busy, who never loses patience and who never ceases to think of the welfare of his children.

> 'Listen to me, O house of Jacob, all you who remain of the
> house of Israel, you whom I have upheld since you were
> conceived, and have carried since your birth. Even to your
> old age and grey hairs I am he, I am he who will sustain you.
> I have made you and I will carry you; I will sustain you and
> I will rescue you' (Isaiah 46:3-4).

Perhaps the most challenging aspect of the divine Fatherhood is his readiness to forgive his wayward children. The sequence of pictures in Luke 15 of the lost sheep, the lost coin and the lost son was designed to show the Pharisees what God is like in contrast to their

own harsh attitudes to 'sinners'. In the process, Jesus shows us God
as a father running to meet his erring but repentant boy:

> '...while he was still a long way off, his father saw him and
> was filled with compassion for him; he ran to his son, threw
> his arms around him and kissed him' (Luke 15:20).

It is amazing, in the light of such a moving example of fatherly love,
that even some Christian parents have been known to disown their
rebellious children and throw them out of house and home. This has
happened even when the children have been repentant. The boy in
Jesus' story was left in no doubt that his father forgave him without
grudge or reserve. There is the pattern, not merely to forgive but to
make that forgiveness transparently obvious. Paul is in harmony
with this example of fatherly love in his instructions:

> 'Fathers, do not exasperate your children; instead, bring
> them up in the training and instruction of the Lord'
> (Ephesians 6:4).

> 'Fathers, do not embitter your children, or they will become
> discouraged' (Colossians 3:21).

As we have seen in earlier chapters, our heavenly Father demon-
strates his love for his children in many other ways. He rescues them
from trouble; he cares for them by providing for all their needs; he
strengthens them and, not least, he loves to talk with them. God also
loves his children enough to train them and discipline them. He does
not spoil them with over-indulgence or by a spineless refusal to
correct or chastise them. All his dealings with his children are wise
and perfectly adapted to the needs of the individual child; this is
instructive for those who are fathers.

Fathers, reward your children

Three times in the sermon on the mount (Matthew 6:4,6,18; see also
Matthew 13:43) Jesus says 'Your Father, who sees what is done in
secret, will reward you'. Here is another element is the example our
heavenly Father gives to human fathers. It is all too easy to

discourage children. This is especially true if a father is strong on corrective discipline; he compounds his mistake of over-emphasis on punishment for wrong doing, with a niggardly attitude when his children do well. Our heavenly Father is not like that. We are right to want our children to be good without bribery, but bribery is one thing, and it is quite another for them to know without a doubt their goodness has been seen and appreciated.

There is a terrible loss of common courtesy at the present time. Children, even those from Christian homes, seem not to be trained to be polite. Perhaps one reason for this is that fathers have forgotten these things and fail to give a good example to their children. Let fathers remember at least to say please when making a request of a child, and to give the priceless reward of thank you, or even better, well done! (Matthew 25:21,23).

If only fathers would realise how great their responsibilities are, and become overwhelmed at the thought of taking them on, they would surely not beget children so carelessly, as many seem to do. On the other hand, let none be discouraged from assuming this privilege, so long as they take our Father God as their example and daily seek his enabling to be good fathers, faithfully loving and guiding the children God has given them.

Church leaders

The Fatherhood of God is not only an example for fathers, it is also the perfect model for church leaders.

The Bible knows nothing of the notion that a church leader should be called 'father'. In fact, our Lord precisely forbids anyone to take that title and to do so is sheer presumption:

> '...do not call anyone on earth 'father', for you have one
> Father and he is in heaven' (Matthew 23:9).

Grace is not mediated to us through the church or its leaders but comes to us directly from the Father by the Spirit through our Lord Jesus Christ. Nevertheless Paul had no hesitation in calling Timothy and Titus his 'sons' (1 Timothy 1:2; Titus 1:4), because it would seem they were converted through his ministry. This same apostle recognised that church leaders need to possess the qualities of a good father, as he demonstrated to the Thessalonians:

> '...we dealt with each of you as a father deals with his own children, encouraging, comforting and urging you to live lives worthy to God...' (1 Thessalonians 2:11-12; see also 1 Corinthians 4:14-15).

There is no room here for authoritarianism or for a harsh judgmental attitude. Rather, Paul gives us an example of a Godlike balance between tenderness and firmness, in his handling of church situations. For example, he says that he was both a mother and a father to the Thessalonian people (1 Thessalonians 2:6-12); and his stinging 'You foolish Galatians' is followed by 'my dear children for whom I am again on the pains of childbirth...' (Galatians 3:1 and 19).

Churches rarely rise higher in spiritual quality than the level of their elders. This leads us naturally on to consider how the Fatherhood of God bears upon the life of a church.

18.
Our Father's family

A church is God's family. This is one of the many pictures given to us in the New Testament to help us understand the nature of church life. Others are a city, a building, a body and a bride. A church is said to be 'the family of believers' (Galatians 6:10), 'God's household' (Ephesians 2:19; 1 Timothy 3:15) and 'the family of God' (1 Peter 4:17).

Founding Father

This was anticipated in Old Testament days when the people of Israel were God's family. God was the Father of Israel in the sense of being its founder, and Moses reprimanded the people on this basis:

> 'Is this the way you repay the LORD, O foolish and unwise people? Is he not your Father, your Creator, who made you and formed you?' (Deuteronomy 32:6).

We sometimes speak of the one who founds a business or a school as a founding father. In the same way the Lord was the founder of the Israelite nation, and Isaiah used this fact to plead with him not to forsake the nation:

> 'Yet, O LORD, you are our Father. We are the clay, you are the potter; we are all the work of your hand. Do not be angry beyond measure, O LORD; do not remember our sins for ever. Oh, look upon us we pray, for we are all your people' (Isaiah 64:8-9; see also 43:1).

This made Israel special in all kinds of ways, she had a special purpose, with special resources to achieve that purpose, but above all she had a special relationship with God himself.

A founding father does not merely begin something; rather his whole mind and heart is in the project. It bears the marks of his wisdom, his energy, his vision and devotion. So it was with the nation of Israel and so it is with God in relation to the church.

We read the story of the founding of Israel in the early books of the Scriptures beginning with the call of Abraham (Genesis 12:1-5), and then on to the Lord's dealings with the nation in the days of Isaac and Jacob, the slavery in Egypt, the Exodus, the wilderness wandering, the giving of the Law at Sinai and their entry into the promised land. This is the account of the Fatherhood of God and how his love, his patience, his power and his wisdom all combined to bring the nation into being.

Because of this relationship Israel could pray for God's forgiveness, restoration and reviving. For example:

> 'Look down from heaven and see from your lofty throne, holy and glorious. Where are your zeal and your might? Your tenderness and compassion are withheld from us. But you... O LORD, are our Father, our Redeemer from of old is your name (Isaiah 63:15).

But sometimes those pleas were not really genuine, as God said:

> 'Have you not just called to me; "My Father, my friend from my youth, will you always be angry? will your wrath continue for ever?" This is how you talk but you do all the evil you can' (Jeremiah 3:4-5).

It is also on the same basis that God promises he will draw his straying people back to himself:

> 'They will come weeping; they will pray as I bring them back. I will lead them beside streams of water on a level path where they will not stumble, because I am Israel's Father, and Ephraim is my firstborn son' (Jeremiah 31:9).

And God frequently reminds them of this relationship:

> 'Is not Ephraim my dear son, the child in whom I delight? Though I often speak against him, I still remember him, therefore my heart yearns for him; I have great compassion for him, declares the LORD' (Jeremiah 31:20).

'A son honours his father, and a servant his master. If I am a father, where is the honour due to me? If I am a master, where is the respect due to me? says the LORD Almighty' (Malachi 1:6).

Not only will they be drawn back to God, but he will multiply their numbers and it will be evident to all around that God is their Father and they are his children.

'Yet the Israelites will be like the sand on the seashore, which cannot be measured or counted. In the place where it was said to them "you are not my people", they will be called "sons of the living God"' (Hosea 1:10).

A new family

All this is a foreshadowing of the founding of the New Testament church of Jesus Christ, and of local churches in particular, as the apostle tells us:

'You are all sons of God through faith in Christ Jesus, for all of you who were baptised into Christ have clothed yourself with Christ. There is neither Jew nor Greek, slave nor free, male nor female, for you are all one in Christ Jesus. If you belong to Christ, then you are Abraham's seed and heirs according to the promise' (Galatians 3:26-29).

The love, wisdom and power of God combined in the sending of Jesus Christ to live, die and rise again for our salvation. The blood of the Passover lamb for the release of the children of Israel pointed ahead to the blood of Jesus Christ poured out on the cross for our release from the penalty and power of sin. So Paul could speak of 'the church of God which he bought with his own blood' (Acts 20:28). Because of all this, a church is not a mere human organisation but a special creation of God for his purpose under his care, covered by his promises, endowed with his power and lavished with his love. He is our Father.

We have already seen that children of God 'participate in the divine nature' (2 Peter 1:4); this fits them for life within the family of God into which they have been adopted. Think of the experience of an adopted child in the early days of life in a new family. It is a new world altogether, with different habits, moral standards, resources, topics of conversation, aims, hopes and fears. Above all, he or she is entering into a relationship with new parents; what do they like? How will they be best pleased? What irritates them? How can love be shown to them? How do they show their love? When God becomes our Father, these are the questions that must occupy us. We will find the answers in the Bible where our Father has made his ways clear. As we become increasingly comfortable with our new relationship we begin freely and gladly to live an entirely different life from what we once were.

We can see now even more clearly why each of us must be born again in order to be a child of God. If we do not share his nature, there is no way we will want to please him, much less will we be able to do so. Even if in a time of religious excitement we begin to enjoy such changes, without the life of God within us the excitement will soon pass and we will resume our former way of life.

One of the family

Imagine becoming a member of a church where all the people are submissive to each other and to the leaders (well, for most of the time!), where they love even those who are not very loveable, where young and old mingle happily together, and where grumbling and gossiping are outlawed. If we were not regenerate we would feel most uncomfortable in such an atmosphere. We might even despise it. This is why it is important to be sure that new members are indeed born again, for the sake of the peace of the church and for the sake of those who ask to be members. No one could possibly be more miserable or a greater problem than an unregenerate member of a local church.

Family life

Since we are children of our heavenly Father, we are to live as brothers and sisters. We are to love one another, as Jesus said:

> 'A new command I give you; Love one another. As I have loved you, so you must love one another. By this all men will know that you are my disciples if you love one another' (John 13:34-35).

Paul likewise:

> 'Now about brotherly love we do not need to write to you, for you yourselves have been taught by God to love each other ... Yet we urge you, brothers, to do so more and more' (1 Thessalonians 4:9-10).

And Peter agrees:

> 'Now that you have purified yourselves by obeying the truth so that you have sincere love for your brothers, love one another deeply, from the heart. For you have been born again...' (1 Peter 1:22-23).

This mutual love according to John, is a sure evidence that we have indeed been born again (1 John 3:14). Our meetings for prayer, fellowship and church business would be transformed if we really put this into practice. We would tremble at the offence we give to our Father when we fail to love each other and even, alas! quarrel and so hurt each other (Malachi 2:10). Here is a marvellous ambition for a church, to be a little piece of heaven earth. We are, or should be, an outpost of heaven in an alien world.

Not only is God our Father, the head of the family, present at our gathering, but our older brother Jesus Christ is also with us:

> 'For where two or three come together in my name, there am I with them' (Matthew 18:20; see also Romans 8:29; Hebrews 2:11).

A family is where we serve one another, and this is no less true of church life (Matthew 20:26-27). We also share together in the work of spreading the gospel. We sometimes become so absorbed in this work that we forget whom we are serving and therefore lose the joy of that service. We need to remind ourselves constantly that while we serve each other and work with each other, we are in fact serving our heavenly Father; it is a family concern (Matthew 21:28-30). This will restore the joy of our service and encourage us to do our very best for him.

There is no greater privilege on earth than being a humble member of the family of God in a local church. There we are fed, encouraged, corrected and guided; there we have the privilege of serving the Lord as we serve our brothers and sisters.

19.
Our Father's image

'Isn't she like her mother!' 'You grow more like your father every day!' Comments like these exasperate teenagers who are struggling to realise their own identity. The odd thing about these remarks is that they are so often expressions of surprise as though the likeness were not the most natural thing in the world. Scattered throughout the previous chapters we have noticed how characteristics of our heavenly Father are to be reflected in his children; it will be helpful now to bring these thoughts together.

As we have seen, true children of God 'participate in the divine nature' (2 Peter 1:4) and something has gone seriously astray if we do not bear to a recognisable extent some resemblance to the family likeness. Either such people's profession to be Christians is a false one, or they are spiritually ill. Physical illness can distort our appearance, and one of the signs of spiritual sickness is a failure to show any likeness to our heavenly Father. This likeness has nothing to do with our physical appearance because 'God is spirit' (John 4:24); rather it is the character of God seen in us. One of the reasons why Jesus Christ came into the world was to show us what God is like. Jesus said:

'Any one who has seen me has seen the Father' (John 14:9)

and the writer to the Hebrews expanded on this theme:

'The Son is the radiance of God's glory, and the exact representation of his being...' (Hebrews 1:3).

This was at least one reason why, at our Lord's baptism, God said:

'This is my Son, whom I love; with him I am well pleased' (Matthew 3:17).

What Jesus did to perfection must be our model.

The family likeness

Nothing pleases our Father more than to see himself reflected in his children. In natural childhood this likeness arises both from sharing our parents' nature and from copying their example. For children of God this is nothing less than the restoration of the image of God in us. That image, once seen to perfection in Adam and Eve (Genesis 1:26;27) has never been entirely lost (Genesis 9:6; James 3:9), but is dreadfully distorted by sin. Now, the work of the Holy Spirit in us ensures that we are being renewed into our Father's image. Two texts in Paul's letters tell us what that image is like:

> '... put on the new self, created to be like God in true righteousness and holiness' (Ephesians 4:24).

> '... put on the new self, which is being renewed in knowledge in the image of its Creator' (Colossians 3:10).

So there are three basic Godlike characteristics that should be seen more and more in our lives.

Righteousness — in this setting means good, honest and happy relationships with other people. In God this is perfectly portrayed in the total harmony between the Father, the Son and the Holy Spirit.

Holiness- this is purity in every part of life, thought, word and deed. It is a total absence of uncleanness and corruption in any form. On this basis God commands us 'Be holy because I am holy' (1 Peter 1:16)

Knowledge — for us this is an understanding of the mind of God and his purposes in the world. Clearly it is not complete knowledge of all things, but children of God grow in their grasp of God's plan for them and, indeed, for the whole universe.

All this is an essential part of the good news of Jesus Christ. Without him, men and women lack these great assets, and because of this they flounder in discord, corruption and ignorance. Jesus Christ puts an end to this confusion and he restores the image of God in those who receive him.

Now let us take a closer look at some Scriptures that speak directly about the ways in which these three character-traits are to be worked out in our lives.

Matthew 5:9

'Blessed are the peacemakers for they will be called sons of God.'

Those who share God's nature will love peace (John 3:17) and do all they can to bring together those who are at loggerheads (James 3:18). Our Father sent his Son into the world to reconcile to himself people who were opposed to him. If we have received the great blessing of peace with God, we will be lovers of peace in the world, in the church, in our family and with our neighbours.

Here, and in some of the passages that follow, the meaning is not that we become children of God by trying to be like him. The reverse is true. We try to be like him because we are his children. When a child shows some characteristic of his or her father, a distinctive habit or a preference for some kind of activity, we sometimes say 'he's (or she's) becoming a real son of his father' by which we mean the family traits are showing more and more clearly. This is the meaning in these texts.

Matthew 5:16

'... let your light shine before men, that they may see your good deeds and praise your Father in heaven'.

God our Father is good, he lavishes upon the world and its people a constant stream of acts of kindness and generosity: 'The LORD is good to all; he has compassion on all he has made' (Psalm 145:9). We are to be good neighbours, renowned for practical help and self-giving for others. This is not to earn the praise for ourselves, but to show others what our heavenly Father is like.

Matthew 5:44-45 (see also Luke 6:35-36)

... Love your enemies and pray for those who persecute you that you may be sons of your Father in heaven...'

In his letter to the Ephesians Paul takes up this theme and expands it (Ephesians 4:32-5:1). The apostle John also tells us that love is the essential evidence of our being children of God:

'... Anyone who does not do what is right is not a child of God; nor is anyone who does not love his brother...We know that we have passed from death to life, because we love our brothers. Anyone who does not love remains in death' (1 John 3:10,14).

Luke 15:25-28

'Meanwhile, the older son was in the field. When he came near the house he heard music and dancing. So he called one of the servants and asked him what was going on. "Your brother has come " he replied "and your father has killed the fatted calf because he has him back safe and sound," The older brother became angry and refused to go in...'

The older brother in this story provides the main lesson. The father of the two boys is a beautiful illustration of our heavenly Father's character as he received back his erring son and forgave him completely despite the fact that he did not deserve it. But the older son knew nothing of the tenderness and compassion of his father. He was harshly self-righteous like the Pharisees who criticised Jesus. He was not a son of his father. He stands as a warning to every professing Christian.

2 Corinthians 6:17-18

'"Therefore, come out from them (unbelievers) and be separate" says the Lord "Touch no unclean thing and I will receive you. I will be a Father to you, and you will be my sons and daughters" says the Lord Almighty .'

Our Father hates evil and loves good. If we bear the same marks, we have an affinity with God and he with us; we are in the family. We are not to isolate ourselves from the people around us. If we do this we cannot share the gospel with them (1 Corinthians 5:10). Jesus Christ involved himself with the 'sinners' of his day (Luke 15:1-2) and our Father never turns his back on his world. But Jesus described our true position in his prayer for us:

> '... they are still in the world ... they are not of the world any more than I am of the world. My prayer is not that you take them out of the world but that you protect them from the evil one' (John 17:11,14-15).

Philippians 2:14-15

'Do everything without complaining or arguing so that you may become blameless and pure, children of God without fault in a crooked and depraved generation...'.

Our Father is pure and holy. The heavenly beings ascribe holiness to him (Isaiah 6:3) and when our Lord Jesus himself spoke to his Father he addressed him as 'Holy Father' (John 17:11).

> Breathe on me, Breath of God,
> Fill me with life anew,
> That I may love what Thou dost love
> And do what Thou wouldst do.
>
> Breathe on me, Breath of God,
> Until my heart is pure;
> Until my will is one with Thine
> To do and to endure.
> (Edwin Hatch).

1 Peter 1:14-17

'As obedient children, do not conform to the evil desires you had when you lived in ignorance. But just as he who called you is holy, so be holy in all you do; for it is written. "Be holy because I am holy". Since you call on a Father who judges each man's work impartially, live your lives as strangers here in reverent fear'.

The world is not our only source of temptation; we also have an old nature with its residue of sinful desires. Peter tells us that God's children control these desires.

This then, is the process through which the work of recreation the Spirit has begun in us will be completed (Philippians 1:6). This completion is certain, as John says 'we shall be like him' (1 John 3:2), and our present responsibility is equally clear 'everyone who has this hope in him purifies himself' (1 John 3:3). The lost image is being restored and this is essential if we are to represent our Father to the world around us. At the same time we are being prepared for our Father's inheritance that awaits us.

20.
Our Father's inheritance

As children of God we belong to a very rich family. We enjoy a high quality of life here and now, and our future is assured; all this is because our heavenly Father has planned that we should share his inheritance. We can understand a little of what our inheritance means by thinking about two ideas that run through Scripture, 'firstborn' and 'double portion'.

Firstborn

The people of God in Old Testament days were called his firstborn:

> '... this is what the LORD says: Israel is my firstborn son' (Exodus 4:22).

Since this applied to the whole nation it had nothing to do with the order in which individual Israelites were born. The idea is borrowed from the fact that a boy who was born first in a family had a position of privilege above the rest. He had a special place at meals and was to be respected by the whole community. He had responsibilities in the family and in the family business, and he had the larger portion of the inheritance. This was the birthright Jacob coveted and which Esau sold to him for a single meal (Genesis 27:1-40; Hebrews 12:16-17). So we see that when Israel was called 'firstborn' it meant that the nation had a special place and great privileges in the purpose and affection of God. Paul listed some of these in his letter to the Romans:

> '...Theirs is the adoption as sons; theirs the divine glory, the covenants, the receiving of the law, the temple worship and the promises. Theirs are the patriarchs, and from them is

traced the human ancestry of Christ, who is God over all, for ever praised! Amen' (Romans 9:4-5).

It is in the same sense that Jesus Christ is called the firstborn (Romans 8:29; Colossians 1:18). This cannot mean, as some have imagined, that Jesus was in some way inferior to the Father. It has no reference to an order of coming into being, but to our Lord's position, privileges and responsibilities. Consistent with this position, Jesus is said to be appointed 'heir of all things' (Hebrews 1:2).

Believers are also called:

> '... the church of the firstborn, whose names are written in heaven...' (Hebrews 12:23).

Furthermore we are united to Jesus Christ by faith, so we share his privileges and his inheritance:

> 'Now if we are children, then we are heirs — heirs of God and co-heirs with Christ, if indeed we share in his sufferings in order that we may also share in his glory' (Romans 8:17).

> '... through the gospel the Gentiles are heirs together with Israel, members together of one body, and sharers together in the promise in Christ Jesus' (Ephesians 3:6; see also Psalm 16:5-6; Matthew 25:34; Luke 12:32; Galatians 3:29, 4:7; Titus 3:7).

For the people in Israel the inheritance was the promised land, but that foreshadowed for them and for us 'a better country — a heavenly one' (Hebrews 11:16). In Jesus Christ we, the firstborn, inherit a special relationship with God and a ready access into his presence now. This is our 'promised land' part of which we inherit now. Later, in addition to this, throughout eternity we will enjoy all the blessings of the new heaven and the new earth (2 Peter 3:13).

Double portion

The second idea we mentioned was 'the double portion'. In Old Testament days the firstborn also received a double portion of the family inheritance (Deuteronomy 21:15-17); no wonder Jacob coveted it! This idea is taken up in Isaiah as a part of the description of the blessings that would come to us through the Messiah, the Lord Jesus Christ:

> 'Instead of their shame my people will receive a double portion, and instead of disgrace they will rejoice in their inheritance; and so they will inherit a double portion in their land, and everlasting joy will be theirs' (Isaiah 61:7).

We see then that the double portion we inherit as the Lord's firstborn is rich beyond measure. The tribe of Levi, from whom the Old Testament priesthood was taken, had no inheritance in the land because the Lord said, 'The Lord is their inheritance' (Deuteronomy 10:9).

> '...You will have no inheritance in their land, nor will you have any share among them; I am your share and your inheritance among the Israelites' (Numbers 18:20).

In this the tribe of Levi represents all the people of God. New Testament believers are all priests (1 Peter 2:9) and therefore the inheritance is for them. What a portion we have! A double portion indeed! The Lord is our inheritance, as the Psalmist enthused:

> 'Whom have I in heaven but you? And earth has nothing I desire besides you. My flesh and my heart may fail, but God is the strength of my heart and my portion for ever' (Psalm 73:25-26).

Not for us the land of Canaan with all its overflowing 'milk and honey' (Exodus 3:8), rather we are to enjoy the spiritual realities which that land pre-figured. Our inheritance includes the great blessings of pardon, peace with God and eternal life. But what is eternal life? Our Lord answered that question when he said 'Now this is eternal life; that they may know you, the only true God, and Jesus Christ, whom you have sent' (John 17:3) How glorious this is, our inheritance is the richness of God himself; we are destined to enjoy his wisdom, his love and his splendour for ever. That is the family treasure, and it is ours.

Our Father's home

In the Bible there are many lovely illustrations of heaven. It is the city of God; it is the throne room of the Most High, it is the control centre of the universe:

'Then the angel showed me the river of the water of life, as clear as crystal, flowing from the throne of God and of the Lamb down the middle of the great street of the city. On each side of the river stood the tree of life bearing twelve crops of fruit, yielding its fruit every month. And the leaves of the tree are for the healing of the nations. No longer will there be any curse. The throne of God and of the Lamb will be in the city and his servants will serve him'
(Revelation 22:1-3; see also Revelation 5:1-5).

These conceptions give us a sense of richness and glory and to them we can add the heart-warming picture of heaven as our Father's home. We have various ways of saying that someone has died; passed on, gone to glory, promoted to higher service; but the most comforting and in many ways the most helpful is to think of dying as 'going home'. This thought is not prominent in the Scriptures but it is there, and first of all in one unexpected place:

'... man goes to his eternal home' (Ecclesiastes 12:5).

We have to admit that the emphasis here is on duration — 'eternal', but there is no reason to abandon 'home' as a most attractive picture of life after death.

When Jesus was comforting his disciples about his departure he said:

'Do not let your hearts be troubled. Trust in God, trust also in me. In my Father's house are many rooms; if it were not so, I would have told you. I am going there to prepare a place for you' (John 14:1-2).

This gives us the impression of a spacious mansion where there is room for all God's children. Here is no cramped hovel, but a place of comfort and liberty. This home is a place of safety where God's children will be secure and at peace. It is anticipated in the Old Testament:

> 'The eternal God is your refuge and dwelling place...' (Deuteronomy 33.27 Amplified Bible).

> 'Lord, you have been our dwelling place throughout all generations' (Psalm 90:1).

Notice in these texts that not only does our Father provide a home for his children, but he is himself that home. The eternal God, the Lord, he is the place of refuge and rest.

This leads us to the last words of Jesus when he died on the cross:

> '... Father, into your hands I commit my spirit...' (Luke 23:46).

Jesus was going home to his Father. After the agony of bearing our sins and his unspeakable separation from the Father, he was now going into the embrace of the loving arms he knew so well. It is true that our experience cannot be the same as our Lord's. No-one took his life from him, as he said:

> 'No-one takes it from me, but I lay it down of my own accord. I have authority to lay it down and authority to take it up again. This command I received from my Father' (John 10:18).

Jesus' death was a positive act by his own power and in his own time — he 'gave up his spirit' (Matthew 27;50). We are not masters of the situation; when we die, the moment and manner of our departure from this life, all is entirely dependent on our Father's will and purpose. Nevertheless, we can still take the dying words of Jesus for ourselves, and as we do so we are saying, 'Father, I am coming home to you, please give me a safe passage and a happy entry into your presence', and we can anticipate with delight the arms of welcome.

Suppose you lived a very long way from home and had never seen your father. The prospect of meeting him one day could fill you with uncertainty, perhaps even with fear. What would he be like? Would he welcome you? Would you be able to relate to him? But suppose your father had frequently written to you; sent messages by other people, and photographs of himself in many situations, and assured you by all these means of his desire for you to come home and live with him. Surely then there would be a tingle of excitement and a feeling of venturing on a new experience; uncertainty and fear would be banished and you would go home to live with a father you already knew and loved, well in advance of meeting him. We have not seen our heavenly Father, but he has made himself known to us his children in very many ways, so that we can say we already know him and cannot wait to go and see him.

Not only so, his Son our Lord Jesus Christ, our elder brother who has loved us, will also be there, as will all our brothers and sisters in Christ. The family of God will be complete and will be united in perfect love and peace and joy for ever. This is our inheritance and when the moment comes for us to join that family circle let this be our prayer, 'Father, into your hands I commit my spirit'.

Bibliography

Behold your God	Donald Macleod	Christian Focus Publications 1990
The Forgotten Father	Tom Smail	Hodder & Stoughton 1980
Children of the living God	Sinclair B. Ferguson	Banner of Truth 1989
Knowing God	J. I. Packer	Hodder & Stoughton 1973

Books by the same author

Born Slaves

Only Servants

The Beauty of Jesus